Chocolate

AND OTHER WRITINGS ON

MALE HOMOEROTICISM

Chocolate

AND OTHER WRITINGS

ON MALE HOMOEROTICISM

Pandey Bechan Sharma "Ugra"

Translated and with an introduction

by Ruth Vanita

Duke University Press Durham & London 2009

© 2009 Duke University Press
All rights reserved
Printed in the United States of America on acid-free paper ⊗
Designed by C. H. Westmoreland
Typeset in Whitman by Tseng Information Systems, Inc.
Library of Congress Cataloging-in-Publication Data appear
on the last printed page of this book.

This translation is dedicated
to Prabha Dixit and Archana Varma

CONTENTS

ACKNOWLEDGMENTS

I am grateful to the University of Montana for granting me a sabbatical that enabled me to work on this project. Thanks to Vani Prakashan, Delhi, for permission to translate from their edition of *Chand Haseenon ke Khutoot*. Many thanks to Archana Varma for help with translating certain words and phrases, and to Saleem Kidwai for reading and commenting on both the translations and the introduction to this collection on very short notice. Thanks to Sadiq R. Kidwai and Frances Pritchett for answering queries, and to Reema Kansal for research assistance in Delhi. Thanks, too, to the readers at Duke University Press, whose comments helped me improve the introduction. I am grateful to my mother for providing the comfortable atmosphere at home in Delhi, where I did much of the work for this book, and to my partner, Monica Bachmann, for very valuable help with the introduction. Any errors that remain are my own.

NOTE ON THIS TRANSLATION

All translations from Hindi and Urdu are by me unless otherwise indicated.

As with any translation, there were numerous difficulties in conveying nuances. Problems arose especially with regard to Sanskritic, Perso-Urdu, and regional language terms for sexual preferences, such as *batukprem, laundebaazi, paatalpanthi*, and with idiomatic turns of phrase, particularly those that involve puns and wordplay, such as Ugra's use of his own pen name and that of the journal *Matvala* as adjectives within the text. In general, I resolve these problems by translating the term or phrase and then providing further explanation in a footnote that appears on the same page as the text.

I translate idioms literally when I judge that such translation adequately conveys meaning, for example, the sense of *murdey par talwar chalana* does come across in the literal translation, "fighting a corpse with a sword." In other cases, I provide an approximation in English, such as *sanaki* as "crazy" or "eccentric," and subsequently explain in a footnote.

Where the resonance of a Hindi term is already widely prevalent in an Indian English term I use the Indian English term, such as "bad character" or "characterless" (*dushcharitra, charitrahin*) for a person perceived as sexually immoral. The stories are liberally sprinkled with quotes from Urdu, Brajbhasha, Awadhi, and Sanskrit, many of which are in verse, and two novel titles are themselves quotes from verse. Where literal translation does not convey the metaphorical meaning of the original phrase, I provide an English saying that conveys the meaning, and provide further explanation in a footnote or elsewhere. Thus I translate *Phagun ke Din Char* as "Life is Brief, Enjoy It" and discuss the connotations in the introduction. I try to retain some of the poetic quality in translation, but where I find the specific wordplay impossible to translate, as in Bihari's "*Harini ke nainan te hari! neekey yeh nain,*" I explain it in a footnote. Nevertheless, many words are heavy with a suggestiveness, which in Sanskrit-Hindi poetics is termed *dhwani*, that cannot be communicated in translation. For example, a *harini* is a doe, but the word "doe," while it is has many poetic associations of its own in English, does not have the lyrical and mystical associations with love that *harini* (or *hirani*) has acquired through centuries of use in Indian poetry and painting.

Except for the word "chocolate," all English words that appear in English script, or transliterated in Devanagari in the original, are italicized in my translation. My own insertions appear in square brackets. All Hindi, Urdu and Sanskrit words that I retain in the original language are also italicized.

The author's use of single and double quotation marks have been adapted to American standards. All ellipses and parentheses are reproduced from the original. I have retained Ugra's stylistic idiosyncrasies, such as his habit of using two or more exclamation points to indicate extreme emotion or of liberally sprinkling third-person prose narrative with the type of dialogue that would normally appear in a drama or film script (both genres he worked in), where the speaker's name is separated from first-person speech with a colon. He also divides stories into sections with no apparent logic — often, in the same story, some sections are marked by numbers and others by asterisks or ellipses. I have retained these stylistic quirks in an effort to be faithful to the original, but also to convey the perhaps uneven terrain of Hindi style in his time.

In all my previous writings on gender and sexuality in India I have followed the practice of spelling Indian language words as close to the way they are commonly pronounced as possible and therefore have not used diacritical marks or transliteration systems. This is because my work is intended for general readers as well as scholars. Many other scholars also now follow this practice.

The fiction appears here in chronological order. The first five stories are in the order in which they appeared in *Matvala* in 1924 (see the prefatory materials), followed by the three that Ugra added in the 1927 book, *Chocolate*, concluding with an extract from his 1927 novel, *Chand Haseenon ke Khutoot* (Letters from Some Beautiful Ones). In *Chocolate*, Ugra arranged the stories in this order: "O Beautiful Young Man," "Dissolute Love," "In Prison," "Chocolate," "Kept Boy," "We are in Love with Lucknow," "Waist Curved like a She-Cobra," and "Discussing Chocolate." But most readers had read the stories in the order in which they appeared in *Matvala*, in 1924: "Chocolate," "Kept Boy," "We Are in Love with Lucknow," "Waist Curved Like a She-Cobra," and "Discussing Chocolate." These five stories are the ones that began the controversy, and they also contain the more ambiguous or even positive representations of homoeroticism. The three new stories that Ugra chose to add to the 1927 book are much more heavy-handed in their negativity. It is no accident that these are also the three stories that do not cite any poetry in homoerotic contexts. My adherence to the original order in which the stories first appeared in print is intended to provide today's reader with a clearer sense of the excitement and horror that first readers would have felt after encountering Ugra's representations of homoeroticism.

Portrait of Pandey Bechan Sharma "Ugra" by Prashant Kumar Nayak from *About Me* by
Pandey Bechan Sharma Ugra, translated with an introduction by Ruth Vanita
(New Delhi: Penguin India, 2007)

INTRODUCTION

The first public debate on homosexuality in modern India took place in the 1920s; it was ignited by a collection of Hindi short stories entitled *Chocolate* (1927) by Hindi nationalist writer Pandey Bechan Sharma (1900–1967), better known as "Ugra," which means "extreme," and can, depending on context, also mean "fierce," "terrible," or "intense."[1]

POLITICAL CONTEXT

Ugra's pen name reflects political conditions in India at the time he began writing. He was in his twenties during the 1920s, when north India was in the throes of the struggle for independence from British rule. Like almost all writers of the time, Ugra was involved both with this struggle and with the social-reform dimension of nationalism. Social-reform movements advocating women's education and rights, widow remarriage, amd Hindu-Muslim amity, while opposing such practices as dowry, untouchability, and child marriage had preceded nationalism in the nineteenth century. These issues continued to both animate and divide nationalists, since the desire for social reform was accompanied by the desire to preserve Indian traditions, and nationalists differed on how this dual task could best be accomplished.

While most Hindi writers were followers of Gandhi, several were right-wing Hindu or Muslim nationalists or left-wing communists, and Gandhians, too, were influenced by these different tendencies. Many were critical, for different reasons, of what they saw as Gandhi's moderate and moralistic methods. For example, in 1922, following mob violence against policemen in a town called Chauri Chaura, Gandhi called off the nonviolent civil disobedience movement that he had inaugurated in 1920. The British rulers then imprisoned Gandhi, and, upon his release two years later, he withdrew from active politics and immersed himself in the constructive movement to end untouchability, uplift women, and improve village life. Many nationalists, like Ugra, were not as thoroughgoing in their commitment to nonviolence as Gandhi was, and saw his decision as an unnecessary setback to the movement. Gandhi did not restart the civil disobedience campaign until 1930.

Hindi men of letters carried on these and other debates through small journals, newspapers, and printing presses, many of which were born, died, and reincarnated in a matter of months. Censors shut down some; others died for lack of funds. Almost all Hindi writers made a living partly as journalists.

The Hindi literary world was also divided on the issue of demarcating the boundaries of Hindi language and literature. One aspect of the Hindu-Muslim conflict, which intensified during the 1920s, was a division between proponents of Hindi and those of Urdu. These two languages were widely spoken, read, written, and understood in north India by both Hindus and Muslims. They are almost identical, except that Hindi is written in the Devanagari script and Urdu in the Persian script, and Hindi draws more of its vocabulary from Sanskrit, while Urdu takes more from Persian and Arabic.[2] Gandhi favored Hindi-Urdu, which he called Hindustani, as the national language, and advocated that all Indians learn both scripts. However, right-wing Muslim and Hindu leaders insisted that Hindi was the language of Hindus and Urdu the language of Muslims.

Even though Hindi and Urdu litterateurs, both Muslim and Hindu, inhabited the same literary and social spaces, the breach rapidly widened during this period. A few Hindus, like Raghupati Sahay, pen name Firaq, continued to write in Urdu, and a few Muslims in Hindi, but most complied with the new pressures. Munshi Premchand, who was inclined toward socialism and was arguably the most popular Hindi novelist of the century, started his career writing in Urdu script but switched over to Hindi script—yet his language, like Ugra's, remained a mix of both.

Both the Hindi and Urdu literary worlds were permeated by a West-phobic indigenism, paralleling Gandhi-led boycotts of imported goods and Western education, yet authors were also, paradoxically, heavily influenced by the West in this period of rapid modernization. A surprisingly large number of Hindi and Urdu litterateurs had studied or even taught English literature at the college level. While they mocked and attacked Westernization, they were also deeply attracted to many Western ideas and institutions. This contradiction is endemic to Indian nationalism and is evident even today throughout the political and literary spectrum. Modern Indian identity remains permeated by anxieties regarding its Hindu, Muslim, and Western components.

These fractures and fusions are evident in the development and reception of the poetry that came to be dubbed *chhayavad*. This was perhaps the most important literary development in Hindi during the 1920s and 1930s; some of the greatest modern poets, including Suryakant Tripathi "Nirala," Sumitranandan Pant, and Mahadevi Varma, were associated with it. These poets and others, such as Maithilisharan Gupt and Makhanlal Chaturvedi, were influenced by the European trends of Romanticism and Modernism, as well as by nationalism and by concern for suffering and oppressed people. Among their greatest achievements, however, was the way they drew on Vedanta philosophy, medieval Indian mystic (*bhakti* and Sufi) poetry, ancient epics, and folk literature to develop a vision of Indic modernity related to, yet distinctly different from, Euro-American modernities.

It was in this environment that Ugra came of age, and all of his early writings are deeply political, nationalist, and reformist in tone. Satire was his favored mode. He rapidly developed a reputation for brazen attacks not only on British rule, but also on such practices as child marriage, dowry, prostitution, Hindu-Muslim animosity, and cruelty to animals. Unlike most of his contemporaries who wrote on these topics, he explicitly described both the disgusting (in a mode termed the *bibhatsa*, or bizarre, in Sanskritic poetics) and the erotic (*shringara*, in Sanskritic poetics) using colloquial and vulgar language rarely used in literary works of the time.[3] In this respect, his work is closer to precolonial, pre-Victorian Indian writing. He delighted in iconoclasm; few writers of the time match his unsentimental depictions of the family, whether urban or rural, as a hotbed of violence, neglect, hatred, sexual depravity, and oppression. It was in this spirit of saying what no one dared to say that he took on the topic of homosexuality.

Chocolate: QUININE OR POISON?

Ugra described his stories about homosexuality as "*undiluted quinine*" and contrasted them with less explicit writings that he termed "*sugarcoated medicine.*" In turn, his detractors called the stories poisonous, claiming that their depictions of vice attracted readers rather than repulsing them. The debate was incapable of resolution, since, apart from its attempt to fix the inherently unfixable meaning of a text, it also turned on the supposed response of readers, a nonquantifiable phenomenon.

The stories were very popular, and while it is impossible to say with certainty exactly why this was so, at least some readers probably did enjoy reading about homosexuality. Gay activist Ashok Row Kavi, founder of India's only nationwide gay magazine, *Bombay Dost*, first drew my attention to *Chocolate* in the late 1990s, when he told me that an elderly gay man of his acquaintance, who was young when *Chocolate* appeared, told him that many male homosexuals had received it with delight. It was this possibility, among others, that Ugra's opponents feared.

Although Ugra claimed that his stories were written solely to expose and eradicate homosexuality, the narratives themselves tell a more complicated tale. Despite the hatred and fear of male-male desire expressed by some of the fictional characters and by Ugra in prefatory materials, the stories nevertheless do give us a picture, however distorted, of urban Indian male-male desire in the early twentieth century. The men engaged in such desire here acquire a local habitation and a name — the stories depict their language, social interactions, even their self-views and self-defense.

It appears that the naming of male-male desire, through a range of terms employed by Ugra, drew opprobrium upon it. When it remains unnamed, as in one of Ugra's novels, *Chand Haseenon ke Khutoot* (Letters of Some Beautiful Ones), extracts from which I have also translated here, and when it is subordinated to male-female desire, the participants can get away with exchanging embraces, kisses, and endearments not very different from those exchanged by the much-maligned protagonists of the *Chocolate* stories.

In his foreword to *Chocolate*, Ugra recounts how he discussed the possibility of writing about homosexuality with other litterateurs, some of whom laughed and told him it was very risky, and others of whom were so embarrassed that they were rendered speechless. "Chocolate," his first story on the topic, was published in *Matvala* in 1924. He claims that, in response to this story, the editor of *Matvala* received "sheafs and sheafs" of letters, both of praise and condemnation. This inspired him to write four more stories on the same theme, published in *Matvala* over the next few months. He was then sent to jail for nine months for editing an anti-British issue of the paper *Swadesh*. When he emerged from jail, his friends advised him not to write any more about homosexuality, as his stories were causing a scandal. This incited him to write three more stories and publish all eight in October 1927, as the collection titled *Chocolate*.

THE MOVEMENT AGAINST OBSCENITY

Banarasidass Chaturvedi, editor of the literary monthly *Vishal Bharat*, published from Banaras, led the campaign against Ugra. Ugra was associated with a rival newspaper *Matvala* (Intoxicated), published twice a month from Calcutta. His stories, serialized novels, poems, and nonfiction appeared in *Matvala*, along with satirical pieces that he wrote for it under pseudonyms, such as Ashtavakra and Aayen Baayen Saayen.[4] The two papers shared a strong nationalist and pro-Gandhi lean but otherwise stood in stark contrast to one another. The contrast is evident in their names, title pages, contents, and style. *Vishal Bharat* (Great India) aimed for a lofty moralism and a high literary tone, while *Matvala* inclined toward colloquialism, satire, and acerbic humor. For example, the February 1929 issue of *Vishal Bharat* carries on its front page the picture of a vast banyan tree, two well-known Sanskrit phrases as epigraphs, and the soon-to-be-famous patriotic poem "Jhansi ki Rani," by female poet Subhadra Kumari Chauhan (1904–1948). In contrast, the title page of the May 10, 1924, issue of *Matvala* emphasizes the irreverent theme of intoxication. It carries a picture of a dancing Shiva, a Hindi couplet by the poet Nirala that uses liquor to symbolize both pleasure and detachment, and a photograph of the young Ugra, who was to be released from British jail the following Monday. The symbolism of liquor and intoxication continues in the way the price of *Matvala* is stated: "One *anna* per cup, three rupees in advance for an annual bottle."

Chaturvedi fired the first salvo in a note with the Sanskrit title "Asato Ma Sadgamaya,"[5] published in *Vishal Bharat* in May 1928. The note accused unnamed litterateurs of adulterating pure ghee (clarified butter, highly prized in Indian cooking and used as a sacred substance in Hindu rituals) with vegetable oil, thereby harming the public physically, mentally, and spiritually.[6] In a subsequent editorial, Chaturvedi used the term *"ghaslet"* for literature he considered obscene. The name stuck, but, paradoxically, the movement he led against such literature over the next two years acquired the title "*ghaslet* movement." *Ghaslet* means "kerosene oil" and suggests inflammatory potential; it also conveniently rhymes with *chaklet*, the Hindi transliteration of Ugra's title *Chocolate*. Chaturvedi somewhat disingenuously denied that he had either kerosene or the rhyme in mind and claimed that in rural areas the word *ghaslet* was used to signify vegetable oil, a product inferior to ghee.[7]

Chaturvedi also insisted that his campaign was not directed against Ugra or *Chocolate* but against obscene literature in general. Another novel dubbed obscene was *Ablaon ka Insaf* (Women's Justice), published by *Chand* (a magazine known for its championship of women) under the female name, Sphurna Devi. Chaturvedi's camp insisted this was a pseudonym for a male writer, and, to illustrate this allegation, *Vishal Bharat* carried a cartoon of a double-headed monster in female clothing, with a man peeping out from behind the woman's head. There is little doubt, however, that the main targets of the *ghaslet* movement were Ugra's writings in general, including his novel about prostitution, *Dilli ke Dalal* (Pimps of Delhi), and *Chocolate* in particular.

Over the next two years, *Vishal Bharat* ran some thirty articles denouncing *ghaslet* literature. *Matvala* issued a couple of rejoinders and also printed a few letters and notes in support of its own position. *Hindi-Punch* and *Navyug* joined in supporting *Matvala*, while *Chand* and *Saraswati* also offered conditional support. Almost every other major Hindi magazine and a number of minor ones jumped into the fray, including *Sudha*, *Marwari Samaj*, *Naya Samaj*, *Pratap*, and *Surya*. Many writers and critics—Padmasingh Sharma, Ilachandra Joshi, Kishoridas Vajpayee, Kalidas Kapoor, Gangaprasad Bhautik, and Ramdas Gaur—were active in the movement against *ghaslet*.

The opponents of so-called *ghaslet* literature argued that it was indecent and obscene because it inflamed rather than extinguishing sexual desires. They advocated writing about sex in a sober and discreet style. In an article entitled *"Ghasleti Lekhakon se Antim Nivedan"* (Final Request to *Ghasleti* Writers), published in April 1929, Chaturvedi expressed displeasure that his print warfare and personal discussions with Ugra and others had proved fruitless, and he threatened to take his movement to the masses if these writers did not mend their ways.[8] He argued that obscene literature had become popular because its writers had taken advantage of the temporary lull in the civil disobedience movement during the 1920s.[9] These writers, he said, would desist only when public assemblies passed resolutions against them, when libraries boycotted their titles, and when the public vigorously opposed booksellers who sold those books. In other words, he intended to use, for purposes of censorship, the weapons of civil disobedience that Gandhi had developed to use against the British government, redirecting these tactics against the speech of ordinary individuals. This misuse of Gandhian tactics, such as the fast (which later metamorphosed into the hunger strike), the boycott, and the sit-in, became rife in independent India.

The debate around whether Hindi should be the Indian national language aided Chaturvedi, because most nationalists wanted literature in the national language to be "pure," both in form and in content. Two major associations dedicated to the spread of Hindi, the Hindi Sahitya Sammelan (Hindi Literature Association) and the Kashi Nagari Pracharini Sabha (Kashi Institute for the Dissemination of Hindi), passed resolutions against *ghaslet* literature. The first of these resolutions explicitly called for using the weapons of civil disobedience to censor the press: "Decent people should boycott such newspapers just as they do foreign cloth and intoxicating substances."[10]

DEFENDING CHOCOLATE?

Only a few intrepid souls dared come to the defense of *Chocolate*, but none came to the defense of "chocolate-lovers" or homosexuals. Most defenders of Ugra argued in sex-phobic and homophobic terms, insisting on artistic freedom of expression only in support of their claim that

Ugra had exercised this freedom in order to reform society and eradicate vice. Both *Chand* and *Saraswati* (the latter was the most prestigious literary journal in Hindi) made this argument.[11] An editorial in *Chand* titled "Ghaslet Andolan" quoted an editorial that had appeared in *Saraswati* in January 1929, arguing that radical young writers like Ugra were intent on exposing vices widespread in society: "One whose character is so weak that he falls into a ditch on reading fiction can be saved only by God! A writer practices his art to benefit society; how can he refrain for the sake of persons of such weak character?"[12]

Ramnath Lal, pen name "Suman" (Flower), made similar arguments in an article "Chocolate and *Paalat*" (the titles of two early stories by Ugra), which appeared in *Matvala* in 1924. This same gentleman later wrote a forty-one-page pseudoscientific essay on homosexuality, which appeared among the prefatory materials in *Chocolate*.

In his 1924 article, Suman argued that boy worship had displaced the worship of the Gods among Indian youth and was rapidly making Indians "lower than animals and flies."[13] He claimed that it was the biggest problem facing India, more important than untouchability, the oppression of widows, or Hindu-Muslim conflicts, since it pervaded all castes, communities, and religions. Suman conceded that some people might be attracted to homosexuality after reading Ugra's stories, but he argued that there was no way to control reader responses of this kind, any more than one could control misuse of scientific inventions: for example, a driver who uses a car to kill someone.

POLITICAL BATTLES: NIRALA, PREMCHAND, AND OTHERS

The controversy was inflamed by personal and political enmities, regional and linguistic rivalries, as well as ideological differences among Hindi litterateurs. Chaturvedi's camp mocked and dismissed not only *ghaslet* but also the new school of *rahasyavad*, which they scornfully dubbed *chhayavad* in Hindi poetry. A foremost exponent was the poet and critic Suryakanta Tripathi (1896–1961), pen name "Nirala" (Solitary/Unique), who also happened to be associated with *Matvala*. Nirala was perhaps the only major writer to defend *Chocolate* in relatively nonhomophobic terms.

Although Nirala, arguably modern India's greatest Hindi poet, was a writer of altogether different caliber from Ugra, their association with *Matvala* placed them, somewhat uneasily, in the same camp, at least temporarily. They and the other young men who worked for *Matvala* had lived in poverty, camping out in the newspaper office and sharing the little they had, whether money or drugs; consequently, they felt among themselves the solidarity of a makeshift family. They saw themselves as iconoclasts blazing a trail, and despised the conventionality of older litterateurs like Chaturvedi.

The *Matvala* camp alleged, perhaps with some justification, that these older authors envied the popularity of younger, more innovative writers. For example, it was said that lines had formed outside Calcutta bookstores to buy *Chocolate*. The first edition rapidly sold out, and the book went into a second edition within weeks.[14] Among the early readers, as mentioned above, were some homosexual men who were happy to find any representation of their lives, even a negative one, although they could not publicly express their appreciation.

Nirala was not so much an impassioned defender of Ugra as a severe critic of people like Chaturvedi, whom he saw as hacks devoid of talent, driven by personal and political antagonisms. He argued for artistic freedom and against the dominance of ideology; this stance earned him the animosity not only of Gandhian nationalists like Chaturvedi but also of the soon-to-be powerful Marxist writers who took over the Progressive Writers' Association.

In a 1933 essay, "Propaganda in Literature," Nirala wrote that propaganda in literature is like salt in a dish — a pinch of it is good, but large quantities are harmful. He contrasted the considered critiques of Mahavir Prasad Dwivedi, a major literary critic and sometime editor of *Saraswati*, with Banarasidass Chaturvedi's campaigns, which he described as nonliterary witch hunts, asserting that the campaign against him (Nirala) had driven him mad. He also noted that Chaturvedi claimed eminence not on the basis of literary talent but by flaunting his friendships with Gandhi and Tagore.[15]

Nirala praised Ugra for his political stories and readable colloquial language — the praise is measured and nowhere suggests that Ugra is a major writer. Noting that *Chocolate* was a popular book, he disputed the idea that Ugra's abandoning fiction for cinema indicated Chaturvedi's victory. He argued that the theme of *Chocolate* could sustain interest only for a short period, and had successfully done so.

Nirala sarcastically remarked that Chaturvedi wanted "originality in his magazine. So he imagined *chhayavad* and *ghaslet* literature into existence—what originality!"[16] In a 1934 essay, he also noted that many critics' personal dislike for particular writers prejudiced them against their writings, and cited the examples of Byron and Oscar Wilde, whose work had been unjustly attacked in their day. Taking a leaf from Wilde's book, he argued that critics should not consider themselves superior to artists or try to fit new art into the straitjacket of inherited norms, because great artists create their own norms.[17]

Nirala was unimpressed by the didactic ideals of purity in literature that appealed to most nationalist writers, including leading novelist Munshi Premchand, who wrote: "I consider the naked portrayal of bad desires in literature very harmful. The best way to combat chocolate etc. is by publishing pamphlets. There is no need to bring it into literature. Literature has a great influence on character. The aim of litterateurs is to build character so one should keep one's ideals and aims pure in this field."[18]

GANDHI AND THE QUESTION OF PURITY

Purity, in the late nineteenth and early twentieth centuries, was a contentious word, both in English and Hindi literary worlds, and both in England and India, as well as in the U.S., where moral crusader Anthony Comstock was one of its chief proponents.[19] It could refer to moral purity, usually a euphemism for sexual chastity, but it could also refer to purity of heart, that is, integrity. It was in this second sense that Thomas Hardy controversially termed Tess Durbeyfield, heroine of one of his most famous novels and an unwed mother, a "pure woman," and also in this sense that poet Firaq Gorakhpuri defended *The Well of Loneliness* as a pure book.[20]

Gandhi had much to do with nationalist constructions of purity, and both camps in the *Chocolate* controversy quoted him to their own ends. While Chaturvedi cited Gandhi's emphasis on sexual purity to attack Ugra, Ugra himself claimed to be reinforcing both that emphasis as well as Gandhi's emphasis on purity as integrity of heart. In his prefatory materials to *Chocolate*, Ugra posited himself as a social reformer telling the "pure truth," with the aim of purifying the hearts of India's youth. The second edition, published in December 1927, carried an appreciative letter from one Sitaram Das, citing Gandhi's article "Plight of School Children," which appeared in *Young India* on September 9, 1926. In it, Gandhi expressed concern regarding masturbation and homosexuality among schoolboys, brought to his notice by a female educationist who described these as rampant problems and claimed that she knew forty-two boys under thirteen years of age who had committed "sodomy."[21] Sitaram Das's intention in citing this article was to show that Ugra, like Gandhi, was trying to expose and eradicate homosexuality among young boys.

But, while both Chaturvedi and Ugra were devoted followers of Gandhi, it was Chaturvedi who was in regular correspondence with the Mahatma. On the other hand, Ugra's closest contact with Gandhi seems to have been when a youthful Ugra and his friend rushed forward to touch the Mahatma's feet as he was walking down a hallway. Chaturvedi took advantage of his association with Gandhi to strike the winning blow. He wrote a note denouncing *Chocolate* and sent it to Gandhi in 1929, along with a copy of the book. Without reading the book, Gandhi published Chaturvedi's letter in *Young India*.[22]

Immediately after this, however, Gandhi read *Chocolate* and wrote to Chaturvedi, "I finished the book today and it did not have the same effect on my mind as it did on you. I think the aim of the book is pure. I don't know whether it will have a good or a bad effect. The writer only arouses disgust at unnatural behavior."[23]

Had Chaturvedi made this letter public, Ugra would have been vindicated, so he chose not to do so. It was only in 1951, in an article commemorating Gandhi's birthday, that Chaturvedi finally published Gandhi's letter attesting to Ugra's purity of intent. He then confessed that when he first received Gandhi's letter in 1929, he immediately set off for Sabarmati to meet Gandhi.[24] He did not discuss *Chocolate* with him, because he knew that once Gandhi made up his mind about a book it was not easy to change his opinion: "So instead of a direct attack, I thought it best to attack in a roundabout manner."[25] He spent forty minutes reading extracts from obscene Hindi literature aloud to Gandhi. He claims that Gandhi said to him, "You did well to come to Ahmedabad. If I had published my opinion, it would have done great harm."[26] Chaturvedi's suppression of Gandhi's letter in 1929 created the impression that Gandhi agreed completely with Chaturvedi; this contributed to Ugra's decision to stop writing fiction for a while and go to Bombay to work in Hindi cinema.[27]

When Chaturvedi finally published Gandhi's letter over two decades later, several critics, including Mohansingh Sengar, editor of the newspaper *Naya Samaj* (New Society), condemned Chaturvedi, accusing him of deceit. Ugra was both outraged and triumphant, and published a third edition of *Chocolate* in 1953, to which he attached a new foreword describing Chaturvedi's revelations along with an article by Sengar entitled "Ek Sahityik Anarth" (A Literary Injustice), which had already appeared in *Naya Samaj* in July 1952, and several letters of self-defense, in a mix of Hindi and English, written by Chaturvedi to Sengar. In his new foreword, Ugra threatened to publish a "white paper" outlining reports on homosexuality from the last twenty-five years (the time that had elapsed between the initial publication of *Chocolate* in 1927 and the third edition in 1953), and to follow it with a short novel entitled *Chocolate Panthi* (Followers of the Chocolate Path). He did not, however, fulfill either of these threats.

FICTION AND NONFICTION: THE ILLNESS AND THE CURE?

Among the more interesting dimensions of the debate was the Chaturvedi camp's argument that nonfiction was the proper arena in which to denounce homosexuality because depicting it in fiction was bound to make it attractive to some people. As mentioned earlier, Premchand had advocated writing about homosexuality in pamphlets rather than in literature. In a long review article, a less known writer, Chandragupt Vidyalankar, took the same view. The three books under review were *Chocolate* and *Ablaon ka Insaf*, both works of fiction, and *Brahmacharya Sandesh* (Gospel of Celibacy), a work of nonfiction by Satyavrat Siddhantalankar. Vidyalankar commences his review with the claim that sexual misconduct pervades Indian society like "germs of disease," and a movement is required to alert the public.[28] However, Vidyalankar argues that an explicit depiction of the illness will result in spreading it. Instead, the topic should be written about in a scientific way, and in a polite style.

Reviewing *Chocolate*, Vidyalankar challenges Ugra's claim that his stories are like undiluted quinine (360). He notes that Ugra himself has titled his book *Chocolate*, not *Quinine*, and alleges that the stories depict "unnatural misconduct" in an "attractive form"(358). He argues that anyone who tries to write fiction on the subject of "chocolate" will find it hard to resist the temptation of including attractive depictions of beautiful boys and explicit descriptions of sexual misconduct: "Precisely because of this difficulty I would commit the impertinence of asking the writer why he developed the desire to write stories on this difficult and delicate topic?" (358). He then contrasts extracts from Ugra's stories, which describe lovers calling beloveds by endearing epithets, kissing, and embracing, with an extract from the nonfictional *Brahmacharya Sandesh*, which uses entirely metaphorical language, figuring lovers as butterflies who suck nectar from flowerlike beloveds and then abandon them to wither in the dust.

Vidyalankar's distinction between fiction and nonfiction breaks down, however, when he considers Suman's essay, "Scientific Analysis of Unnatural Fornication," which is among the prefatory materials attached to *Chocolate*. Although this is nonfiction, he objects to Suman's quoting excerpts from explicit autobiographical materials by homosexual men, such as J. A. Symonds, extracted from books by Havelock Ellis and other sexologists. He assimilates Suman's essay to fiction by saying that it is written in an entertaining style, as if the author is telling grandmothers' stories to children by a fire on a winter's night. He once again holds up as a model the dire warnings issued in *Brahmacharya Sandesh* against masturbation, homosexuality, prohibited types of marital sex, and adultery. The author of this book also uses Havelock Ellis but, according to Vidyalankar, instead of literally translating the text, he summarizes it in restrained language.

Perhaps the most revealing part of Vidyalankar's essay is a metaphor he uses towards the end to contrast fiction about homosexuality with nonfiction on the same topic: "It is certainly not a bad idea to expose this filth, but those who present filth in an attractive form should keep in mind every moment that this 'filth' attracts the hearts of ordinary humans like a magnet, so it should be exhibited with a sense of responsibility. The hygiene inspector of a city supervises its cleaning, and the *bhangi* [sweeper-caste person] who cleans latrines also comes in contact every day with filth, but there is always a difference between the viewpoints of these two. The *bhangi* cannot keep himself apart from filth as the inspector can" (364). Apart from contempt for sweepers as inevitably dirty people, the passage also reveals Vidyalankar's view, accepted by all parties to the debate, that human beings naturally incline to same-sex desire as they do to many practices considered filthy, such as masturbation. Although participants in the debate borrowed the term "unnatural" from British discourses on homosexuality, their discussions suggest that they consider homosexual relations both attractive to humans and polluted, like many other attractive but dirty things. Their revulsion stems from the feeling that homosexual relations are dirty and shameful and cause loss of "caste" and class, rather than from the belief that such relations are unnatural.

Ugra's own attitude towards caste was somewhat more complicated. In his memoir *Apni Khabar* (About Me) (1960), which is considered the first modern autobiography in Hindi, and which I have recently translated, Ugra sharply condemns Brahman corruption and states that although he himself was born in a Brahman family, he has, from birth onwards, always been a Shudra.[29] Quoting the *Manusmriti's* dictum that all human beings are born Shudras and acquire higher caste status only through initiatory rites that constitute a second birth, Ugra argues that since he never underwent such rites, he has remained a Shudra, which, according to this formulation, is the basic human condition. Ugra praises this unshaped condition as replete with potential. He argues that just as a piece of stone can be carved into an image of any deity, but an icon of Shri Krishna cannot become an icon of Radha, so also a human in the Shudra condition can become anything, but a person of any other caste is constrained by an inflexible condition. In terms similar to those of Renaissance philosopher Pico della Mirandola in his famous essay "On the Dignity of Man," Ugra claims, "As long as I am unformed, any form and all forms are in me."[30]

Sarcastically pointing out that supposedly pure Brahmans also are humans, and excrete bodily wastes, Ugra says he finds Shudras more attractive than Brahmans and enjoys their company, preferring dirty, crowded marketplaces and wandering itinerants to domesticity. In a similar vein, Nirala, in his 1932 essay, "*Sahitya mein Charitra*" (Character in Literature), discusses modern litterateurs' obsession with pure moral "character" and argues that only one born of an *ayoni* (non-vagina) could possibly be pure.[31] God, says Nirala, has forestalled discussions on pure character by fashioning the pathway into and out of the womb, whereby we all share in impurity.[32] Pointing out that Indian literature always portrays even the greatest humans, like Sita, as flawed, he attacks the hypocrisy of those who, like the proverbial crane (*bagula bhagat*), pretend to be meditating ascetics until a fish comes within reach.

EVERYBODY LOVES CHOCOLATE?

The word *chocolate*, which Ugra, in his foreword, claimed to have invented as a synonym for the popular term *laundebaazi* (boy chasing), rapidly came to be used by everyone in the debate, including supporters and opponents of Ugra, as well as indifferent parties like Nirala. Today, this connotation of the word is no longer widely known, but from the mid-1920s to the mid-1930s, it functioned in the Hindi literary world as a convenient code word that enabled avoidance of more explicit language.

In Ugra's first story, "Chocolate," the narrator's friend offers a definition that was much quoted in the ensuing controversy: "'Chocolate' is the name for those innocent, tender, and beautiful boys of the country, whom society's demons push into the mouth of ruin to quench their own lusts."

Vidyalankar had a point when he asked why Ugra had chosen the word chocolate, rather than poison or quinine, as a title. The type of chocolate favored by Indians tends to be sweet, rich, and milky, not bitter. Given the long Indian tradition of celebrating the virtues of milk products, such as ghee, butter, and cream, the popularity of chocolate in India is not surprising. While underlining the supposedly Western origins of male-male desire, the term chocolate to some extent normalizes that desire because chocolate is almost universally popular. It simultaneously indicates how ineradicably Western tastes are part of modern Indian identity.

It may be relevant that chocolate has erotic and mildly aphrodisiac qualities.[33] Oscar Wilde, whose writings were popular in early twentieth-century India, often depicts his young male protagonists, including Dorian Gray, "discussing" (Victorian English for "consuming") a cup of chocolate.[34]

Chocolate is one of the most widely available consumer items in India; it is so indigenized that its name has become a Hindi word, yet it is non-Indian in origin, compared to Indian sweetmeats like laddoos. Is a taste for chocolate therefore non-Indian, and less moral than a taste for laddoos? The absurdity of this question indicates how the word chocolate works against Ugra's narratorial denunciations of homosexuality. It suggests that an attempt to eradicate homosexuality in modern India would be as self-defeating and anti-pleasure as an attempt to eradicate the taste for chocolate.[35] Debates around sexuality in modern India thus were and are inextricably intertwined with debates about colonialism and nationalism, the Western and the indigenous. When I recently gave a talk on Ugra at a workshop in India, a woman activist who works with a sexuality rights organization in New Delhi told me that "chocolate" is still used as street lingo among some groups of non-English speaking homosexual males to refer to an attractive effeminate man or boy.[36] Other words they use, like halwa and mitha, also refer to sweetmeats; like chocolate, these are sweet, sticky and desirable objects. This is exactly the way the term is used in Ugra's stories—by more "masculine" males to refer to more "feminine" and beautiful males who are objects of desire. It appears likely that Ugra did not invent the term chocolate, but briefly brought a subcultural code word into wider circulation. The other possibility is that Ugra did invent the term and it filtered down to homosexual men, who began using it thereafter. I incline to the first possibility, because Ugra claims an unvarnished realism for the stories in which he depicts men using the term, and defines it for the naïve narrator.

COLONIALISM AND THE NEW HOMOPHOBIA

Saleem Kidwai and I have traced the history of modern homophobia as it developed in nineteenth-century colonial India, manifesting itself in laws, medical, and educational policies, and in the rewriting of literary canons in Indian languages.[37] A homophobia that was marginalized and ineffective in precolonial society became dominant in the course of the nineteenth century, especially among the educated classes. This new homophobia was one manifestation of a modern Puritanism imported from Victorian England. Reacting defensively to British administrators' and missionaries' assaults on Indian sexual mores as promiscuous and idolatrous, and on Indian men as effeminate, Indian social reformers and nationalists claimed that Indian society was and always had been sexually purer than British Victorian society itself.

From the late nineteenth century onwards, Hindu adherents of new reformist sects, such as the Brahmo Samaj and the Arya Samaj, insisted that authentic Hinduism had always been both monotheistic and monogamous. Litterateurs, both Hindu and Muslim, launched purification campaigns to clean up precolonial Indian literatures; for example, Muslim reformers tried to remove the tropes of love and wine from Urdu poetry, and successfully if superficially heterosexualized the *ghazal*, or love poem.[38] In his prefatory essay, Suman commends Urdu for cleaning up its act, pointing out that the Urdu and Persian *ghazal* traditionally depicted male-male desire and also conventionally gendered both lover and beloved male until reformers like Muhammad Husain Azad (1830–1910) began to purify it.

Such reformers also suppressed Urdu *rekhti* poetry, a genre that, up to the first half of the nineteenth century, had freely depicted women's sexual lives, including their lesbian relationships.[39] Similarly, Hindu litterateurs denounced and excised from the canon much erotic medieval poetry in Hindi, Sanskrit, and Bengali, including *riti* poetry of the seventeenth and eighteenth centuries, and erotic treatises descended from the *Kamasutra*, such as the *Anangaranga* and the *Ratirahasya*. Modern Hindi translations of these treatises frame them as texts warning against impurity and giving advice to married couples.[40]

Sex manuals warning against masturbation, premarital and extramarital sex, and homosexuality multiplied. A good example is the Urdu *Do Shiza* (Virgin), by Hakim Muhammad Yusuf Hasan.[41] The author, who claims to be a doctor (*hakim*), insists that this is not a religious text, but rather a medical one, intended to give readers knowledge of the body and of sex. Claiming that popular sex manuals derived from the Hindu *Kamasutra* are salacious and unreliable, he discusses masturbation and homosexuality in some detail, issuing dire warnings about how these practices ruin the health. He claims that a woman who has sexual relations with women soon starts looking as if she suffers from tuberculosis. This absurd idea appears to have been prevalent at the time, because Ugra depicts boys developing tuberculosis as a result of homosexual relations. Hakim Hasan recommends that parents police young children, monitor their time in the bathroom and in bed, and prevent them from reading romantic fiction or spending unsupervised time with friends, whether of the same sex or the other sex. Such manuals appear to have borne some relation to increased policing by authority figures; for example, Ugra approvingly recounts in his memoir how the headmaster of his school used to rebuke boys for walking with their arms around one another, growing their hair long, or dressing in fashionable styles considered effeminate.[42]

Male homosexuality was a particularly touchy issue for modern educated Indians, because, in the course of the nineteenth century, it had become strongly associated in England with effeminacy. Indian men, as subjects of colonial rule, and especially after the revolt of 1857 was crushed, were particularly vulnerable to the charge of deficient masculinity.[43] Despite these anxieties, it is significant that no public spectacle of persecution on the scale of the Wilde trials took place in India, although several writers and public figures were widely known to be homosexually inclined.

Nevertheless, by the time Ugra's stories were published, the new Puritanism and homophobia were well entrenched among all sections of the national movement, from the Gandhian to the Hindu, the Muslim to the Communist, and thus among the urban, educated middle classes. While manifested primarily in silence on sex-related issues, censorship of erotic materials, and advocacy of premarital celibacy, these attitudes were also evident in campaigns to reform courtesans and sex workers as well as singing and dancing women, many of whom were accomplished artists (*devadasis* and *tawaifs*).[44] Reform, in this context, referred not to improving working conditions for these women but to moral reform of the women themselves. Reformed women were expected to repent of their evil ways, abandon their profession, and either get married or take up work considered respectable, such as needlework, which could be done at home. Even though such work generally brought in a lower income, it was considered superior because it was moral and because it moved women from the public to the private sphere.[45] Significantly, both governmental and most nongovernmental agencies in India today, including many feminist organizations, continue to espouse a similar line regarding sex workers, even though sex workers themselves have begun to organize and demand legalization of their profession and better working conditions.

These moral concerns regarding sex were part of a larger puritanical approach to life. Nationalists of all stripes shared a highly censorious approach to fashion, especially women's fashion, as well as to dancing, theater, cinema, nondidactic fiction, and anything that seemed oriented towards pleasure for its own sake.[46] The term *Westernization* often functioned, and continues to function even today, among both right-wing and left-wing nationalists, as a code for selfish sensuality and self-indulgence. Nationalists' virulent denunciation of homosexuality, on the few occasions when they discussed it, was just one dimension of a general anti-pleasure and anti-sex philosophy. With regard to homosexuality in particular, though, the Western legacy of terming it unspeakable created a strong countertendency to refrain from discussing it, even for purposes of denunciation. The impulse to silence any mention of homosexuality and the impulse to denounce it collided in the controversy around Ugra's writings.

Ugra was attacked for two reasons—for his choice to break the silence around homosexuality, and for his deeply ambivalent depictions of homosexuality. Not only does chocolate as a symbol for male-male desire suggest that the desire is as ubiquitous as the delicacy, but Ugra depicts this desire as deeply embedded in happily hedonistic lives led amid urban pleasures. Ugra's stories represent the homosexually inclined man as a sort of everyman about town, a modern version of the *nagaraka* (city dweller) who is the protagonist of the *Kamasutra*—he is urbane, educated, pleasure-loving, attracted to beauty in either sex, and familiar with Indian as well as Western literatures.

In the West, today, the view of homosexuals as a minority with a clear-cut identity, whose sexual preference is probably fixed at birth or very early in life, has largely displaced the view that anyone may, some time in life, be attracted to a beautiful person of the same sex. Contrary to Michel Foucault, David Halperin, and others, who argue that this modern Western view of homosexuality as an orientation is a nineteenth-century European invention, both views in fact coexist in ancient and medieval Indian texts.[47] Saleem Kidwai, examining networks of homoerotically inclined men in precolonial Indian cities, such as Delhi, suggests that both views coexisted in those societies too.[48]

Ugra uses "chocolate" to refer both to a male's male love object and also to a taste, preference, or inclination. A chocolate lover is one who likes to eat chocolate but also one who has a predilection for chocolate in the abstract. Ugra's chocolate lovers love particular males whom they term their "chocolates," but they also have a taste for male love in general.

In the stories, the view of male-male desire as *any man's* natural response to beauty coexists with the view of *some men* as more given to this desire than others, and of such men as comprising a group whose worldview is inflected by their desire for males. For example, schoolteacher Prasad, in *"Hum Fidaye Lakhnau"* (We Are in Love with Lucknow), has been homosexual since his youth, and invokes a group identity when he tells the shocked narrator, "My people's goal in life is happiness. We will try to enjoy ourselves even in hell."

On the other hand, many characters in Ugra's writings view desire for beautiful males, like desire for beautiful females, as a natural and logical result of loving beauty and pleasure: that is, the outcome of an aestheticist and hedonistic way of life. Mahashayji, a poet, tells the censorious narrator, "Truth must be respected wherever it is. Beauty alone is truth. So whether the beauty is a woman's or a man's, 'I am a slave of love.'" Ugra's friend, Suman, in his attempt to scientifically analyze homosexuality, takes a similar view, quoting Havelock Ellis to argue that beauty is the visible cause of attraction and all beauty is intrinsically feminine—hence the propensity of men to ignore masculine women but to be attracted to feminine women or feminine men. He thus characterizes same-sex desire as intrinsically human because it is based on aesthetics and emotion rather than sex drive alone, and he claims that other animals are free from it, even though he also dubs it unnatural as well as bestial.

This self-contradictory view of same-sex attraction is not a simplistic one—it leads to several questions. Is it natural for a male to admire and love male beauty? Does this love become a problem only if it takes the form of sexual activity? Are certain erotic acts between men permissible—for example, kissing and embracing—while others, such as anal sex, are forbidden? Or are all erotic acts between men vicious? Suman ties himself up in knots trying to answer these questions, and Ugra's stories fail to provide definite answers. For example, in "O Beautiful Young Man," the protagonist denounces any type of eroticism between men; he beats up a youth whom he finds sitting in a park with his arm around a boy, and he warns other youths who gather round not to let any man kiss or embrace them or address them with endearments. But even though this unnamed protagonist functions, in one sense, as the moral center of the story, he is referred to throughout as "*sanaki*" (eccentric or crazy), which casts some doubt on his opinions.

If we look beyond *Chocolate* at other writings by Ugra, the waters become even more muddied. In his 1927 novel, *Chand Haseenon ke Khutoot* (Letters of Some Beautiful Ones), the Hindu hero has an affair with a Muslim woman but also has an equally if not more intense romantic friendship with another man, who is single. The "beautiful ones" whose letters compose Ugra's epistolary novel are both male and female. The two male friends always address one another as *"Priyatam"* (Dearest) and *"Pyare"* (Beloved); they recall with delight their youthful romantic friendship, and their exchanges of endearments and embraces. The hero falls in love with a Muslim girl, whose chief attraction appears to be her uncanny physical resemblance to his male friend. When he kisses her, he tells his friend to be prepared to lose caste, because he will kiss him too. In response, his friend says that he will shave off his beard and become smooth-skinned in preparation to be kissed and embraced, because he knows that his friend is a worshiper of beauty. Ugra depicts this intensely erotic, if not explicitly sexual, friendship in altogether celebratory terms, and nowhere hints that there is anything wrong in the two men kissing, embracing, or using romantic endearments to one another. Even the endearments are the same. For example, in the story "Chocolate," Dinkar addresses his beloved, Ramesh, as Pyare. The fact that one man is in love with a woman suffices to legitimize the romantic relationship between the two men.

Phagun ke Din Char (Life Is Brief, Enjoy It), a novel published in 1960, is similarly complicated. It depicts homosexual and heterosexual liaisons as equally immoral or amoral, and as part of a hedonistic life-style, both in the traditional urban center, Banaras, and in the modern urban center, Bombay. The novel's title, *Phagun ke Din Char*, is similar to *Chocolate* in its ambivalence. Derived from a song by medieval woman mystic Mirabai, the phrase literally means, "the month of Phagun has only four days," but idiomatically advocates enjoying life's pleasures (including the erotic pleasures of the Saturnalian festival of Holi, which falls in the month of Phagun), because life is short.[49] The gesture towards hedonism in this idiom is similar to that in the Latin tag, *carpe diem, carpe florem*, or its English equivalent, "Gather ye roses while ye may."

Ugra's depiction of pleasure and hedonism as options even for married, middle-class, educated men was a daring one in its context; it evokes the specter of the married, homosexual Wilde and his hedonistic characters like Lord Henry, who corrupt the young. In choosing to depict middle-class men who prefer men rather than female situational homosexuality (secluded women turning to each other when men are not available), Ugra goes against the trend of modern Indian fiction.

This reversal of a trend emerges too in Ugra's depiction of male-male relationships as not just about sex but also about love. Urdu woman writer Ismat Chughtai's depiction of female-female sex in her story "*Lihaf*" (The Quilt), for which she was put on trial for obscenity in 1944, provides an instructive contrast. "*Lihaf*" tells the story of a spurned wife who has sex with her maidservant and, when the latter is away, tries to molest the narrator, a young girl who is visiting her. The word *love* never appears in "*Lihaf*." The relationship between the two women is only about sex, not love. They never claim to be in love or use endearments to one another. The mistress uses the maid to satisfy her cravings, described as an itching disease, and the maid exploits this need to obtain the privileges of a favored servant.

In Ugra's stories, homophobic characters like the narrator challenge the validity of male-male love, yet the homosexual characters repeatedly assert that they are in love. They also act like conventional romantic lovers—pining, sighing, composing and reciting poetry, offering gifts, and pursuing the beloved.

Both Ugra and Chughtai raise the bogey of pedophilia (an issue I discuss in greater detail later in this introduction), but Ugra's homosexual characters are allowed more agency, a more assertive voice, and, most important, are depicted as preferring men to women even when women are available, while Chughtai's protagonist turns to her maid and the narrator only after her husband rejects her in favor of boys.

MASCULINITY ON THE DEFENSIVE

As I have demonstrated in earlier work, Indian fiction, in the modern era, before the development of overtly gay and lesbian writing from the 1970s, reverses a premodern dynamic of gender representation.[50] Premodern Indian literatures tend to represent male-male desire more often than female-female desire. In the modern period, both male and female writers focus far more often on female than on male homosexuality. This is largely because modernity reshapes earlier, more androgynous, Indic ideals of masculinity and instead posits it as the polar opposite of femininity, attempting to erase the shared middle ground. When male homosexuality does appear in modern literature, it is usually relegated to the underworld of prisons, slums, and criminal gangs, where it is depicted as caused by the absence of women.

Perhaps *Chocolate* aroused such great hostility because it reversed that paradigm. Except for one story set in jail, none of Ugra's protagonists belongs to the underworld. They are respectable members of society—teachers, college students, writers—who carry on their affairs both in public and in private. Nor is their homosexuality premarital and thus explicable by a lack of options. Many of them are married.

Even more important, the protagonists are not isolated neurotics. Although some of their male acquaintances condemn their desires, several others are supportive and view such desire as a natural response to beauty. Both in "Kept Boy" and in "Waist Curved Like a She-Cobra," male friends bond around collective attraction to a beautiful boy, who becomes their communal object of desire. The atmosphere of shared desire, where men incite one another with poetry, song, and exclamations to pursue and woo an attractive youth, is reminiscent of Dargah Quli Khan's description of eighteenth-century Delhi, where men gaze on youths in public places and organize concerts where the youths sing and dance to entertain their admirers.[51]

In each of the eight stories, the narrator expresses hostility to male-male desire, but when he enters into a debate with homosexually inclined characters, he never wins on logical grounds and has to fall back on visceral disgust. The narrator is an ambivalent figure who engages in morally dubious conduct, such as eavesdropping (in "We Are in Love with Lucknow"), and turns against his friends as much from personal pique as from moral outrage (in "Waist Curved Like a She-Cobra"). This ambivalence is perhaps best depicted in the figure of Shivmohan in "Kept Boy." Shiv shares his friends' admiration of the beautiful boy and actively helps protagonist Mahashay with his plans to befriend the boy, but later denounces homosexuality to the narrator, even while acknowledging, "In this matter, I consider myself weak like Mahashayji."

The narrator sometimes compromises, and advises discretion to a friend who is determined to pursue an affair with a male. More often, he summons authority figures to his aid. Though he may succeed in punishing the homosexual, it is clear that he does not eradicate homosexual activity. In two of the eight stories the lover is defamed and leaves town; in one he loses his job and is later imprisoned; in one he is driven to suicide by public embarrassment; in one the beloved dies of tuberculosis, supposedly induced by homosexuality, but the lover goes unpunished; and in one the lover is beaten by the police and frightened into silence.

Of the remaining two stories, one is set in jail, where two men fighting over a third are punished, but it is clear that homosexual behavior is uncontainable; the other takes place in a men's college, where it is equally clear that the principal's rebuke of the students has no effect whatsoever. Characters in the stories emphatically state, as does Ugra in his preface, that homosexuality in the prison and men's college is not situational, but rather is representative of homosexuality prevalent throughout society.

The last story, "*Chocolate Charcha*" (Discussing Chocolate) is framed as a self-reflexive debate among passengers in a train, some of whom like *Matvala* while others loathe it. The debate is not about homosexuality alone, but also about Ugra's stories themselves and the question of whether homosexuality should be a topic of public discussion. A defender of *Matvala* exclaims, "Many great poets, writers, and even political leaders are said to be suffering from this sickness." Ugra repeatedly hints that his stories are based on personal experience, and his characters are thinly veiled portraits of men he knows.

Chocolate thus paints a picture of Indian masculinity as almost irrevocably compromised by all-pervasive homoeroticism. The hedonistic protagonists of *Chocolate* consider their masculinity enhanced, not diminished, by their desire for other males, but this older view is contested by the newer idea that homosexuality signals deficient masculinity.

In the 1920s, modern media such as magazines displayed a good deal of anxiety about masculinity, along with intense interest in sexual pleasure and prowess. *Matvala*, in which Ugra's stories first appeared, is replete with advertisements for products to enhance virility and the pleasures of sex. For instance, a 1925 issue carried two ads that together occupy a whole page — one for an illustrated book titled *Kashmiri Koka-*

shastra, published in Punjab, which promises full satisfaction to *vilasis* (hedonists), and the other for a medication to cure impotence, distributed from Calcutta.[52]

Despite these anxieties, older traditions of passionate intimate friendships as well as playful flirtation between men also persisted well into the twentieth century, as is evident from looking at the letters of virtually any male writer or public figure of the time, including Ugra. For example, Shivpujan, an admirer of Ugra's, writes to him, praising *Chocolate*, and says it has angered homosexuals; however, the terms in which he depicts this anger are ambivalent: "Some boy worshipers would crush you like sugarcane if they caught you alone." Shivpujan then remarks that those who have not met Ugra and seen his "lovely form" (*manjul murti*, literally "sweet icon") cannot fully appreciate his writings. The letter playfully ends, "Well, on your way, do give me one 'kiss.'"[53] Another litterateur writes, "I will love you a lot — don't worry, it won't be *unnatural*."[54]

THE QUESTION OF "BOYS"

Ugra's depictions of male-male desire are ambivalent in at least one other way: there is a slippage between his opposition to all homosexual desire because he considers it unnatural in itself and his frequent equation of male homosexuality with man-boy desire, what has today come to be called pedophilia. The stories frequently lament the supposed damage caused to the physical and psychological development, health, and education of boy beloveds, who are corrupted by older men and become homosexual as a result.

But the "man" and the "boy" are usually not very far apart in age — the lovers in Ugra's stories are mostly young men in their late teens or twenties, while the beloveds are mostly younger males between the ages of thirteen and seventeen. There are several exceptions to this pattern, and Ugra notes that beloveds are called "boys" (*laundas*), regardless of age. In the story set in prison, the narrator realizes that a beloved "boy" may turn out to be sixty years old! As John Boswell has pointed out, "boy" and "girl" function as endearments in erotic contexts, and are often unrelated to age, as is seen in words like boyfriend and girlfriend.[55] It must also be remembered that the definition and understanding of childhood in Ugra's time differed significantly from their definitions among today's urban middle classes.[56] The age of marriage varied regionally and by community, but many men of Ugra's generation were married by the time they were fourteen and most women much younger, between the ages of eight and fourteen. Marriage in early teens or even younger continues to occur in parts of rural India. Gandhi married and had sexual relations with his wife when both were thirteen; this was typical for men of his community. Nirala was married at eleven and began living with his wife when he was sixteen and she thirteen. Men in their twenties, thirties, and forties, whose wives died in childhood or in childbirth, were often remarried to girls from the age of eight upward.

The legal cases that ignited battles among nationalists over the question of fixing a legal age of consent to sex in marriage concerned girls of eight and under.[57] Many nationalists were unwilling to change the laws even to protect girl wives under ten. In this context, the furor over boys of fourteen having sex with boys between the ages of seventeen and twenty is attributable more to homophobia than to child protection.

Homophobia combines with an overvaluing of males and an undervaluing of females to make it acceptable for younger girls, but not younger boys, to be sexual objects for older males. Thus, in his novel, *Chand Haseenon ke Khutoot*, Ugra refers to the heroine, a teenage college student involved in a heterosexual love affair, as a *balika* (girl/girl-child), but far from considering her too young for romance or marriage, he celebrates the fact that she abandons her education to commit herself to her male lover. In *Chocolate*, however, when Ugra uses the male equivalent, *balak* (boy/boy child) to refer to male teenage beloveds, he laments these boys' predicament, because he considers them too young for love.

Contrary to the stereotype still dominant both in India and in the West today, not all male-male relationships in India or other non-Western countries function along the axis of man-boy, older-younger, active-passive, lover-beloved, nor did they always function in this way in the past. Although he uses these stereotypes to homophobic ends, Ugra does depict other kinds of homosexual relations too. In "Dissolute

Love," the man-boy relationship is finally exposed because the boy is caught having relations with another boy of his own age. In "Discussing Chocolate," adult college students woo and seduce one another – age difference plays no role here, although good looks do. The warden of the student dorms confesses his inability to intervene because the boys are adults. In "In Prison," prisoners fight over handsome adult men.

THE "CHILDREN IN DANGER" ARGUMENT IN INDIA TODAY

Although the 1920s controversy around Ugra's stories is long forgotten, many of the irrational prejudices and absurd ideas bandied about in the debates of that time are still alive and well, and continually resurface in today's debates about sexuality, obscenity, censorship, and the civil rights of gay people. Most important among these is the common homophobic tendency to confuse adult consensual male homosexuality with the molestation of male children. Ugra's stories are rife with this confusion, and it persists today, especially among Western-educated men and women in powerful positions in Indian academia and government.

Pedophilia is constantly cited as a reason to retain Section 377 of the Indian Penal Code, a law introduced by the British in 1860, which makes "unnatural intercourse" (generally interpreted as homosexual, particularly male-male intercourse) a crime punishable by up to ten years' rigorous imprisonment.[58] This outdated law remains on the books in India, although its progenitors, the British, have removed it in their own country, as have all other major democracies. The law has recently been challenged in India as a violation of civil rights guaranteed in the Constitution, and the petition is currently being heard by the Delhi high court.[59] A few years ago, LGBT groups, women's organizations, and human rights groups in Delhi discussed strategies to eliminate Section 377. These discussions broke down because while some LGBT groups wanted Section 377, with its unpleasant associations, to be removed from the Penal Code, and Section 376, the antirape provision, reworded to include man-boy rape, some women's organizations insisted that Section 377 be retained in a changed form and expanded to include all forms of adult-child molestation, including female manual and oral abuse of female children. Some lesbian groups objected to this, because it would mean that lesbianism would for the first time be mentioned in Indian law, but only in a criminal context, while both lesbians and gay men continue to be deprived of civil rights.

The major difference between the debate in Ugra's time and that in our own is the visibility of lesbian and gay organizations, especially of anti-AIDS organizations, in India today. As a result of LGBT movements, both in India and abroad, the English-language Indian media is now, by and large, sympathetic to gay people's struggles for civil rights. The media in other Indian languages, however, remains somewhat more ambivalent.

The struggles of poor and uneducated people inclined to same-sex desire generally emerge into media visibility only when their lives are on the line—when men are arrested for consorting with each other, and when female couples are illegally arrested for living together or are driven to suicide by family and police violence.[60] While the visible LGBT movement and its sympathizers are often criticized for being Western-educated and urban, what is forgotten is that the vocal opposition to homosexuality also comes primarily from Western-educated urban nationalists—right-wing, left-wing, and centrist—who hold positions of power and whose arguments are almost identical with those made by nationalists in the 1920s.[61]

Pedophilia often works as the trump card of such homophobes. In April 2005 and again in January 2006, I was invited to be on two television talk show panels in New Delhi that discussed Section 377 in the context of its misuse to harass gay people. While most members of the audience opposed this law, a senior police office, known for his work in children's rights organizations, defended it, on both occasions. Initially, he claimed he wanted to retain the law to protect boy children from rape, because antirape laws are worded to protect only females. But when the show's host asked whether he would favor scrapping Section 377 if another law were introduced to protect male children, he demurred, saying that 377 protects "victims of homosexuality" against "sodomizers." He also compared homosexuality to theft and murder. His mildest statement on the subject was that homosexuality is a sickness and should remain illegal, but that all homosexuals should be helped. A young, gay, Hindi-speaking man in the audience pointed out that he was in no need of help, because his family had accepted him, and he intended to stand for political office as an openly gay man. In another vein, a feminist lecturer at a Delhi University college, who was participating in an all-women feminist workshop in which another scholar and I presented papers on same-sex pleasure in texts and media, claimed that such discussion might legitimize gay men's hypothetical interest in molesting her six-year-old son.

This confusion between adult consensual homosexual relationships and child rape is imported into India from the West. It has proved perhaps the most popular of all homophobic arguments thus imported, because it is one of the very few arguments not based on the Bible. Unlike the West, India does not have any extended precolonial tradition of persecuting people for same-sex relationships, and the majority religion, Hinduism, has no significant history of condemning or proscribing homosexual relations. Hinduism's many sacred texts, traditions, and teachers disagree on many issues, including homosexuality.[62] Those modern, educated Indians who wish to justify homophobia must therefore do so on secular grounds, which is very hard to do. Given the size of India's population, it is hard to claim, for example, that nonprocreative relationships are harmful to society (although the Shiv Sena women's wing made a valiant attempt, claiming that the film *Fire* might incite all women to be lesbians, thus halting population increase).[63] Hence the popularity of the pedophilia argument, calculated as it is to arouse moral panic among the middle classes.

SEXUALITY AND BOY ACTORS

With one exception, all the relationships in *Chocolate*, whether between adult men or men and boys, are consensual and based on seduction. The exception occurs in "Waist Curved Like a She-Cobra," when a boy actor is molested against his will but with his father's consent.

This is significant, because it evokes Ugra's own childhood experiences. Ugra was born into a very poor Brahman family in the village Chunar, Uttar Pradesh. His father died while he was a baby. He was named Bechan ("sold") to avert the evil eye, because several of his siblings had died in infancy. In his autobiography, *Apni Khabar* (About Me), which is still unmatched for frankness among Hindi writers' memoirs, Ugra narrates how his older brother sold household goods to finance his drinking, drug use, and gambling, and kept prostitutes in the house. He regularly battered his wife, his mother, and the child Bechan.

During his father's lifetime, Bechan's two older brothers had begun to act in Ramlila performances (religious dramas based on story cycles of the life of epic hero Ram, incarnation of preserver God Vishnu) in the town of Mirzapur. Their father tore them off the stage and brought them home, but after his death they went back to acting. Bechan was given the role of Ram's wife Sita in the village Ramlila, and when he was eight or so, his brother sent him to Banaras to act in a theater company there. In his novel, *Phagun ke Din Char*, Ugra depicts the theatrical life of Banaras as corrupt and licentious.

His brother then joined an itinerant religious theater group that traveled all over north and northwest India, and took Bechan along with him as a boy actor and his unpaid servant. Bechan was taught to sing, dance, and walk with a sway. He describes how he used to put vaseline in his long hair so that it smelled like the perfume used by prostitutes. He played the role of Ram's wife Sita, and at other times of Ram's younger brothers Lakshman and Bharat. Ugra describes how thousands of men and women touched his feet, when, at the ages of eleven and twelve, he played these deities. He jokingly remarks, "He who has not had a wife all his life, had become Ram's wife in the early years of his life" (38).

The boy actor who is molested in Ugra's story "Waist Curved Like a She-Cobra" is a Gujarati and acts in Parsi theater in an urban center, not Hindu religious drama in rural areas or small towns.[64] But, like Ugra, he plays female parts.[65] The narrator voices the conventional reformist sentiments of the time when he denounces Parsi theater as obscene. Reformers considered the suggestive songs, dances, and dialogs of Parsi theater obscene, but they did not condemn Hindu religious drama, which was viewed as indigenous rather than Western, traditional rather than modern, and morally edifying rather than simply entertaining.

Ugra breaks down this simple opposition when, in his memoirs, he presents an insider's view of itinerant religious theater in north India in the first two decades of the twentieth century. The experience was formative for him in more ways than one. It was here that he acquired knowledge of Tulsidas's *Ramcharitmanas*, a sixteenth-century retelling of the Ram story that is still the most popular version of the epic in north India today. Tulsidas ever after remained one of his two favorite poets, the other being the nineteenth-century Urdu poet Ghalib.

Backstage life for the participants in religious theater was permeated by eroticism of different kinds, and intoxicants were freely imbibed. The boys who acted in these plays were called *murtis* (icons). The term, like its Urdu equivalent, *buth*, had an erotic connotation, because the actors were love objects for both men and women. Rumors were rife that Pathans (tribals in northwest India) kidnapped handsome boys; the head of the theater group, Mahant Bhagwatdas, was also suspected of seducing boys when he took them into his bed to warm them after cold baths early in the morning. Ugra opines that this was just the "unperverted tender side" of the generally hot-tempered Bhagwatdas's personality, and not a cover for sexual activity (47).

Later, Bechan and his two brothers joined another group headed by Mahant Ram Manohardas. Unlike the first group, in which most of the actors were *sadhus* (religious mendicants), most of the members of this group were professional actors. Ram Manohardas would patronize and seduce handsome young actors, who would then also fall prey to other men in the group. Ugra claims that he escaped seduction because his two older brothers protected him (50). Not everyone believed this claim.[66] At the age of twelve, Ugra fell in love with a beautiful seventeen-year-old girl in the audience at the village of Barabanki, in Uttar Pradesh, as did many men from the company. She accepted a sari from Ram Manohardas and also contracted a venereal disease. When her husband found out, he tortured her to death (51).

Ugra's life did not always conform to his moral pronouncements; therefore, it is not surprising that that some people suspected him of homosexuality. For example, his fiction and his foreword to *Chocolate* denounce drinking, drugs, gambling, and prostitution but, like Nirala and other members of the *Matvala* group, he was notorious for openly drinking, taking opium, and gambling.[67] He mocked those who did not take opium and made arrangements to obtain it even when he was in a British jail.[68] Although he was extremely pugnacious and sooner or later fell out with nearly everyone with whom he came in contact, Ugra, as a middle-aged man, had a following of young writers who took opium in imitation of him.[69]

His sexuality remains something of a mystery. While one acquaintance recounts that Ugra and two friends took a vow of celibacy, others say he was not celibate but enjoyed the "market of beauty," although he never engaged in adultery.[70] He enjoyed watching dancing girls perform and mentions that he fell in love with "a semiprostitute," while an older married prostitute fell in love with him (*About Me*, 141). Fellow writers describe him as a dandy, fond of wearing perfume and garlands.

Just as Ugra's denunciations of drinking, gambling, and dancing girls were performed in fiction rather than life, so also his denunciations of homosexuality have a strongly theatrical quality. This is suggested by the tropes he uses, including the invocation of the *sutradhars* of government in his foreword to *Chocolate*. The *sutradhar* is the stage manager and principal actor in traditional Sanskrit and Hindi drama, who often introduces the play; a puppet master is also called a *sutradhar*. Ugra goes on to recount how he decided to break the silence around homosexuality by writing *Chocolate*: "I thought to myself, Very well. It is I who will take this *risk*. I will play this unpleasant part in an unpleasant play." If all the world's a stage, Ugra's self-chosen part was that of a pugnacious contrarian, a hero to some and a villain to others.

THE LOVE OF BEAUTY

Ugra was himself suspected of being homosexual, perhaps because his narrator in several stories seems like a persona. The narrator has experiences the author was known to have had (for example, being a political prisoner or writing for *Matvala*). Most of his friends appear to be homosexually inclined; also, Ugra claimed that the stories were based on real-life experiences. As he recounts in his foreword, several friends warned him that his stories were causing him to be defamed: "People are criticizing you and calling you 'frivolous,' '*launda*,' 'chocolate,' and who knows what else. . . . When the whole society wants to keep quiet about it, why are you so anxious to play with fire?"

Ugra was a lifelong bachelor, and his writings betray an odd mixture of conventional nationalist didacticism with an unconventional, almost antinomian, aestheticism and hedonism. Most late twentieth-century Hindi literary critics carefully avoid addressing these contradictions and simply defend Ugra as an outspoken denouncer of "unnatural misconduct."[71] These unabashedly homophobic critics, themselves professors at major urban universities, ignore the ambivalences in Ugra's portrayal of homosexuality and continue the earlier convention of florid denunciation: "Ugra produces disgust for same-sex fornicators and denounces this misconduct as inhuman and accursed."[72] These critics use the term *samlingi rati*, which now appears in Hindi dictionaries as a translation of "homosexuality" but was not in use in the 1920s when the *Chocolate* controversy occurred.

Mohanlal Tiwari is the only recent Hindi critic who, while contrasting Ugra's realism with the idealism of other writers, complicates this assessment (albeit somewhat confusedly): "Ugra's true guru in realism was the nakedly realist British writer Oscar Wilde. He considered beauty the symbol of all symbols. . . . The collection of stories, *Chocolate*, is influenced by Oscar Wilde. There is plenty on this theme in Urdu verse as well."[73]

FOLLOWER OF WILDE?

While it would be hard to claim Ugra as a follower of Wilde on the basis of *Chocolate* alone, some of his later writings reveal a shift in his views on art and morality. In a 1940 essay, *"Adarsh Upanyas"* (The Ideal Novel), he writes, "I look first for pleasure in a novel, even if it has no message and no utility." Answering critics who find his works too passionate, he argues that passion (*josh*) constitutes the power of art and then proceeds to list which writers, in his view, have this passion and which lack it: "This is the same passion which is in Oscar Wilde, but he has a unique way of expressing it. Passion that survives is power, so only one whose writings have lasting passion is a powerful writer."[74]

Ugra comments in more detail on Wilde's life, work, and fate in his 1960 novel, *Phagun ke Din Char* (Life Is Brief, Enjoy It), in the context of discussing a character named Liladhar, a gifted dance teacher whose womanizing and attempts to prostitute his wife drive her to suicide, and who sells his son to men, one of whom ends up murdering the boy.

Ugra argues that Liladhar is a great artist like Wilde but is, also like Wilde, "*langot ka kacha*" (literally, of immature underwear, a metaphor discussed in more detail in the next section), that is, given to promiscuous sexual pleasure and willing to indulge himself with both men and women.

In *Phagun ke Din Char*, written towards the end of his life, Ugra tempers his critique of homosexuality with an analysis of art and pleasure that is worth quoting at some length:

> "All the arts are immoral," said—perhaps—the strange, characterless, but great English-language artist Oscar Wilde. Oscar Wilde's inner artist was of the form of fire. It digested everything—heads or tails, straight or bent. The art not just of Oscar Wilde but of any artist worth the name becomes like fire when it attains maturity. Any accomplished artist has an infinite capacity to absorb and digest both purity and impurity. Most humans readily engage in worldly misdoings. It is only natural for humans to be drawn to pleasure. Any art grows, matures and becomes intense through hard work and austerity.[75] But it decays, grows distorted, and rots through gratification and pleasure.[76] Some of Wilde's works are so beautiful that one feels like kissing the author's pen![77] I agree with the many who think that Oscar Wilde's writings are much superior to those of the famous Bernard Shaw. In my opinion, if the Goddess of talent was pleased with both of them, she was charmed by Wilde as a mistress is, and by Shaw as a mother is. The artist in Shaw is far removed from enjoyment: no soap or cigarettes; no flesh, wine, or women. If Shaw were not a comic writer, he would be considered a sage.[78] In the company of pleasure-loving artists, black as crows, Bernard Shaw appeared white as a crane.[79]
>
> But the artist in Oscar Wilde, the God who dwelt in him, was the ultimate artist, Krishna. At the melodious notes of his sweet flute playing, his accomplished artistry, every pleasure-loving civilized woman became his girlfriend, and every pleasure-loving male youth his boyfriend. Do you know, sir, the meaning of *sakha* (boyfriend)? *Sa* means "with," and *kha* means "eat": bread bitten by teeth![80]

Ugra's figuration of Wilde as Krishna is highly evocative. Early twentieth-century Indian nationalist writers tended to exalt the monogamous Rama above the playful Krishna, even though both deities are incarnations of Vishnu. For example, Pandit Madhavacharya, in his 1934 introduction to his 1911 Hindi translation of the *Kamasutra*, discusses sexual desire but mentions only the philosopher-king Krishna of the *Gita*, not the later Krishna who was the lover of Radha and the other milkmaids.[81] Instead, he denounces adultery and claims that monogamous sex with one's wife is the only lawful kind of sex, citing Rama as the model of such love.[82]

Conversely, Ugra compares Wilde to Krishna and adds a playful mock-etymology of the word *sakha* (boyfriend): "*sa* means 'with' and *kha* means 'eat': bread bitten by teeth!" Ugra's use of this word is interesting because in devotional literature and commentary, Krishna's male friends, the cowherds, are called his *sakhas*, but any possible eroticism in their connection is seldom mentioned.[83]

Ugra goes on to reflect on the effect that the Wilde catastrophe had on the literary world:

> For decades after Wilde's disgrace and punishment, respectable British and European men, who cleverly hide their own vices, thought it a sin to touch his immortal works! The last days of this God of art were spent in exile, far from his birthplace and his dear ones, in a hell of poverty and sickness.
>
> The world eats sugar with clarified butter, but Wilde ate clarified butter alone. Most artists are careful to swallow when they are underwater. The fish of crime and punishment does stick in their throats, in the painful form of sickness, failure, and grief, but they escape society's wrath. Because he was an openly and unashamedly pleasure-loving artist, Oscar Wilde's disgrace and ruin was perhaps unmatched in the history of art. . . .
>
> But I want to return to Oscar Wilde's claim that all art is immoral. Do you agree with this claim? I would agree with it because morality is the daughter of law, and stays within bounds, while art can never, in any age, accept curbs or restraints. So how is it possible for art to be anything but immoral?[84]

In contrast to his writings from the 1920s, where Ugra justified his writings about sex by claiming that his aim was to purify society, here he declares his agreement with Wilde that art cannot accept any restraints, and therefore is amoral. Accordingly, he portrays Liladhar, despite his misdoings, as a complex character rather than an outright villain—a true artist who wins laurels for his art.

Nor does Ugra excuse licentiousness only in artists. In *About Me*, he recounts the amorous adventures of a married male friend. In his youth, this man was enchanted for years by the "well-formed body" of a young male hockey player (131); later, he fell in love with a female prostitute and also had an affair with his wife's younger sister; furthermore, he was sporting enough not to interfere when his wife had an affair with his own younger brother. Ugra remarks, "I very much like such youthful men, despite their vices. Who is without 'vice'? Only God" (133).

TERMS OF DESIRE: CREATING A LANGUAGE

If Ugra saw vice as ubiquitous among humans, this may partly explain the gusto with which he engaged it. He may be credited with creating and accessing a minor lexicon of terms relating to male-male desire. On the one hand, he uses general terms normally used in heterosexual contexts: for example, one story is titled "*Vyabhichari Pyar*" (Dissolute Love). The word *vyabhichar* applies to any kind of illicit sex and is most commonly used to refer to heterosexual adultery. Here, however, it is used to refer to the married protagonist's love for a boy. Similarly, he uses the generic *bura kaam* (bad act) to refer to homosexual acts.

Somewhat more ambivalent is the term *yaar*. Commonly used in modern colloquial Hindi as the equivalent of "buddy," "pal," or "friend," the word has an illustrious poetic heritage, both hetero and homoerotic, with the meaning "male lover," derived in part from Sanskrit *jara*, a woman's adulterous lover, a history of which Ugra would have been aware. In his stories, male friends use this term in a nonerotic way, but when they are depicted as bonding around shared homoerotic desire, the word *yaar* becomes erotically charged.

Apart from "chocolate," Ugra's characters use the code terms "pocket-book" and "money order" to refer to an attractive male. More research is needed to determine whether these terms were actually in use at the time. He also uses the terms still common today, such as *launde-baaz* (boy chaser/fancier) and its derivative, the abstract noun *launde-*

baazi (boy chasing) as equivalents for homosexual, and refers to *laundas*, "boys," who may even be sixty years old. While *launda* is an Urdu word, Ugra also occasionally uses the Hindi equivalent *larka* and the Sanskrit *batuk prem* (boy love). *Buth* (idol), the Urdu poetic term for a beloved, also appears.

Homosexually inclined men are termed "chocolate *panthi*" (literally, followers of the path of chocolate) and on occasion *paatalpanthi* (followers of the path of *paatal*, which is a rose or trumpet flower). The term *panthi* is a suffix conventionally attached to the name of a sect or a teacher, thus a Kabir *panthi* is a devotee who follows the path (cult or sect) of medieval mystic Kabir. Ugra's use of it constructs homosexuality as a way of life, and almost a religion.

Ugra follows the Western practice of using ellipses to indicate sexual acts between men, thus rendering them unnameable; however, on one occasion, he uses the dialect term *ghokhana*, derived from Sanskrit *ghoshana*, meaning "to cry aloud" or "to proclaim," to describe what boys learn to do in darkened rooms. This evocative word seems to suggest cries of pleasure (or pain) during sex acts.

In other writings, Ugra uses the phrase "*langot ka kacha*" to refer to homosexuality or bisexuality; for example, in his memoir, *About Me*, he describes Ram Manohardas, director of the theater group in which Ugra worked as a child, as *langot ka kacha* because he slept with boys. *Langot* is a loincloth worn as underwear, and *kacha* means "raw," "uncooked," and, by implication, "immature." Other terms Ugra uses, less pejoratively, are *sarvabhogi* (taking pleasure in or consuming everything) and *ranginmijaaz* (of colorful temperament), an Urdu term that has a history of connoting same-sex desire.[85]

Above all, poetry, especially Urdu poetry, functions in Ugra's works as a language for male-male desire. Here, homosexual protagonists and the avowedly homophobic author are on the same page—both quote Urdu verse to set the tone for the narrative. Thus, "Kept Boy," which contains the largest number of verse quotations, has as its epigraph an Urdu couplet about the many dimensions of love.

It is therefore appropriate that the city of Lucknow, the historical locus of so many poetic traditions, is invoked as site and signifier of pleasure, especially homoerotic pleasure. In the story "*Hum Fidaye*

Lakhnau" ("We Are in Love with Lucknow"), the homosexual Prasad, who relocates to Lucknow after studying in Delhi, sings a verse, "Lucknow is in love with us, / We are in love with Lucknow." The city of Lucknow, and the province of Avadh of which it was the capital, have a long and rich history of celebrating transgressive desires, ranging from the power of courtesans and the cross-dressing of kings to male-male and female-female eroticism.[86] This haunting verse about a cultural love affair between Lucknow and an undifferentiated "we" (lovers of beauty? homosexuals? hedonists?), which the narrator triumphantly claims to have silenced at the end of the story, but which Ugra reinscribes in the title, resonates both with the past and the future of same-sex love.[87] That past is marked both by Hindu and by Muslim cultural practices, which explains why many modern Indians and Pakistanis are uncomfortable with it. Ugra depicts his homosexual characters as very much at ease with this mixed heritage, and indeed with a hybrid international heritage.

CONTESTED ANCESTRY: HINDUS, MUSLIMS AND THE WEST

The *Chocolate* debate is part of a modern Indian debate, extending from the nineteenth century to the present, about the sources of modern Indian identity. A central question in this debate is: how do Hindus, Muslims, and "the West" constitute or undermine this identity? Ugra's homosexual protagonists unabashedly claim an ancestry that crosses space and time. In the title story, protagonist Dinkar Prasad quotes the famous Urdu poet Mir Taqi Mir's homoerotic love poetry, but he also looks to the West for inspiration: "He said that Shakespeare too was the slave of a beautiful friend of his. He also talked of Mr. Oscar Wilde."

If Shakespeare, like the trope of chocolate, signals the Western component of modern Indianness, the *ghazal* or Perso-Urdu love poem signals its Muslim component. Almost all Ugra's "chocolate lovers" are Hindus, but they constantly quote Urdu *ghazals*, and some even compose them. These quotations inspire appreciative listeners to respond with quotations from Hindi erotic poetry. In Ugra's stories, canonical poetry by great Indian poets like Mir and Bihari functions as the cultural glue that bonds homoerotically inclined men and also bonds

Hindus and Muslims. Interestingly, the homophobic narrator rarely quotes verse.

In Uttar Pradesh, where Ugra grew up and where the Hindi literary establishment was based, most litterateurs were (and are) given to quoting *ghazals* at the drop of a hat. Ugra's depiction of his openly homosexual protagonists claiming as their own this high literary tradition, supposedly spiritual in its orientation, generated extreme anxiety among the literati.

Instead of depicting homosexuality as a foreign import, Ugra highlights its hybridity, and also the hybridity of Indianness. He accurately represents his young men about town as a group comprising both Hindus and Muslims, most of whom are fluent in Hindi, English, and Urdu. They speak the kind of language that Gandhi termed Hindustani, a mix of Hindi and Urdu, sprinkled with many English words, phrases and sentences. Today, this is the language of urban India, on streets, in homes, in cinema and on television.

Ugra blames the Western education system, with its residential schools and universities, for encouraging same-sex desire; one character goes so far as to say that he would kill his son rather than allow him to be educated in this system. However, by the early twentieth century, the Western education system was too deeply entrenched for middle-class Indians to see its eradication as either possible or desirable. Many of those who denounced *Chocolate* had children studying in these educational institutions, which is likely to have heightened their anxiety.[88]

The denouncers of *Chocolate* were thus caught in a contradiction. On the one hand, they associated homosexuality with the West, and viewed any discussion of it as a Western innovation that would corrupt Indian society. On the other hand, the terms in which they expressed their homophobia were drawn directly from Western sources. For example, in August 1929, *Vishal Bharat* approvingly published a translation of Professor Gilbert Murray's March 23, 1929, letter to the editor of the British newspaper, the *Nation*. This letter, arguing against obscenity in literature, appeared in the course of a six-month-long debate in the *Nation* generated by the 1928 British ban of Radclyffe Hall's lesbian novel, *The Well of Loneliness*. The hybridity of Hindi writers was exemplified by their closeness to the British literary world, which enabled Murray's letter to be translated into Hindi within five months of its initial publication.[89]

The prefatory essay to *Chocolate* by Ugra's friend Suman is a prime example of this contradiction. As his bibliography and extensive quotations indicate, his knowledge of homosexuality, as well as his homophobic analysis of it, are based entirely on sources in English and French, ranging from Havelock Ellis to Balzac, Darwin to the *Encyclopaedia Britannica*. However, he claims that although homosexual relations may have occasionally occurred in ancient India, knowledge and widespread prevalence of same-sex relations was transmitted from ancient Greece to both Europe and west Asia, and imported into India by Muslims in the medieval period.

"The West," homogenized by the nationalist imagination, constituted a component of modern Indian identity that nationalists, Hindu and Muslim, found perhaps even more difficult to accept than the Muslim and Hindu components. They acknowledged its presence in modern India primarily as a subject of complaint, lament, or diatribe.

GANDHI AND TAGORE:
THE LARGER DEBATE ON "WESTERNIZATION"

The debate on homosexuality reflected this larger national debate on India's relationship with the West. A famous discussion on this theme took place between Mahatma Gandhi and Rabindranath Tagore. These two mutually devoted friends, who were also probably the two Indians best known in the West, conducted intermittent discussions in public forums, first in 1921, and then again from 1928 through the 1930s. Tagore's comments generally appeared in the nonpartisan nationalist magazine *Modern Review*, and Gandhi's in his own magazine *Young India*. The debate turns on the value of pleasure for its own sake, also central to debates about homosexuality.

As Ramachandra Guha points out, Gandhi's famous pronouncement—"I do not want my house to be walled in on all sides and my windows to be stuffed. I want the cultures of all the lands to be blown about my house as freely as possible. But I refuse to be blown off my feet by any"—was "squeezed out of a reluctant Mahatma by Rabindranath Tagore,"[90] and is immediately preceded by the statement, "I hope I am as great a believer in free air as the great Poet."[91] The difference between their attitudes was relative, not absolute, but nevertheless significant.

Tagore disapproved of Gandhi's denunciations of modern machinery and factory-based production, and especially of the campaign in favor of homespun and against foreign cloth, which took the form of burning foreign clothing and of what Tagore saw as Gandhians' fetishization of the spinning wheel. Disagreeing with Gandhi's desire to return to village-based production, Tagore, like Wilde, argued that man was made for something better than drudgery: "If the cultivation of science by Europe has any moral significance, it is in its rescue of man from outrage by nature . . . the all-embracing poverty which has overwhelmed our country cannot be removed by working with our hands to the neglect of science" (104).

Tagore was suspicious of purity that required negations, and therefore of Gandhi's advocacy of poverty and celibacy. Tagore interpreted Vedic philosophy as advancement towards joy (*ananda*), with *Om* signifying "the everlasting yes" (57), and contrasted it with Buddhist and Gandhian emphases on suffering and self-abnegation. He feared that Gandhi's followers' self-repression, unlike that of Gandhi himself, was based on fear rather than affirmation, and would easily morph into violence against dissenters. He predicted that nationalism would not tolerate freedom of expression and gave the example of nationalist protest against a newspaper editor who had mildly criticized the burning of foreign cloth: "How long would it take for the fire which was burning cloth to reduce his paper to ashes?" (78).

While deeply critical of modern Western civilization, Tagore also felt that India's greatest civilizational attainment, the perception of oneness in difference, would be undermined by nationalist hatred and fear of the West: "The idea of India is against the intense consciousness of the separateness of one's own people from others . . . India has ever declared that Unity is Truth, and separateness is *maya*. . . . Our present struggle to alienate our heart and mind from those of the West is an attempt at spiritual suicide" (61).

The same issues—pleasure versus duty, hybridity versus purity, and diversity versus uniformity—were at stake in the Hindi literary debate around sexuality in general and homosexuality in particular. Poet Suryakant Tripathi Nirala, Ugra's fellow writer at *Matvala*, was one of the very few Hindi litterateurs who did not take a puritanical moralistic stance on these issues. Nirala's nationalism, like Tagore's, drew on an internationalist vision. Nirala translated and commented on the works of writers in Sanskrit, Urdu, Bengali, English, and modern Hindi and its predecessors such as Avadhi and Brajbhasha; his subjects range from Blake, Shelley, Vidyapati, Tulsidas, Bihari, Ghalib, Insha, and Mir to contemporary poets, especially Tagore, whom he deeply admired.

Like Tagore, Nirala consistently advocated the study of world literature and judged "*ekdeshiya*" (mono-national) writing "inherently narrow."[92] Nirala disagreed with those nationalists who felt that world friendship could develop only after India became independent, or that literature must be censored to conform to nationalist ideals. "Unbridled litterateurs and literature are equally useful to the country, society, one's own religion, other religions, and the world," Nirala claimed.[93]

Narrowness, Nirala thought, was also evident in the critical desire to confine creative writing in generic, moral, and ideological bounds. He argued forcefully in favor of hybridity and intercourse among different literary traditions: "Those regional languages that are considered strong and rich have attained this superiority through the advent of ideas from outside. Those ideas have caused their own ideas to shine in hundreds of forms and colors, like the many beautiful colors of the rainbow in the rays of one sun."[94]

Nirala mocked those who attacked erotic writing on the grounds that it would offend Indian women's purity. In a 1928 essay, he translated late medieval Bengali devotional poetry, replete with Krishna-Radha eroticism, to demonstrate that explicit depiction of the body and of sexual activity was not a new or modern development, and argued that people with inflexible intellects could not appreciate the ever-changing beauty of art.[95]

Nirala's nonjudgmental approach to sexuality emerges in his 1939 novelette, *Kulli Bhaat*, a sketch of his long friendship with Pandit Patwaridin Bhatt, nickname Kulli. This work of fiction provides a suggestive contrast to *Chocolate*. Nirala is a rebellious sixteen-year-old when he is sent to fetch his wife from her village.[96] Kulli, a twenty-five-year-old, fashionably dressed in the style of Lucknow, and notorious in the village for reasons not clear to Nirala, befriends him. Nirala defies his in-laws in order to meet Kulli alone, and Kulli courts him in conventional fashion with compliments, sweets, betel, perfume, and garlands. Nirala does not initially understand what is going on, but he likes the way Kulli looks at him: "I had never experienced such a look before. I was curious, and also pleased" (271). Nirala rejects Kulli's sexual advances but remains his friend.

In contrast to Ugra, who depicts teenage boys as victims corrupted by men in their twenties, Nirala relates the same kind of encounter from the boy's point of view. Instead of being outraged, Nirala is puzzled, amused, and pleased. In his brief foreword, he says that his character acquired breadth from contact with Kulli, who was "first and foremost a human being, who will always be honored from a human point-of-view" (270).

Ugra violently denounces hidden homosexuals in the Hindi literary world as vicious hypocrites; Nirala, in his dedication of *Kulli Bhaat*, notes their existence, apparently looking forward to a day when they will be able to declare themselves: "I did not find anyone in Hindi literature worthy of this novelette's dedication. Although many share Kulli's qualities, all are afraid of those qualities being brought to light. Therefore I postpone this dedication."[97]

An interesting dimension of Nirala's depiction of male-male love is that he shows it coexisting with another taboo kind of love: that between Hindus and Muslims. Later in life, Kulli falls in love with a Muslim woman, and Nirala advises him to defy society and marry her. When Kulli dies, although he is a Brahman, no priest is willing to perform his obsequies. Nirala, also a Brahman, performs the funerary rites. A similar nexus of desire, although less explicit, is found in Ugra's novel

Chand Haseenon ke Khutoot, where, of the two male characters who are passionately devoted to one another, one falls in love with a Muslim girl and the other declares that if he ever marries, he may perhaps marry a widow or a girl from another religion or caste. Once the line of propriety is crossed, transgressive desires multiply, a possibility that creates moral panic among some readers.[98]

Kulli Bhaat stands alone in Hindi literature of its time, and even today, for its sophisticated and sensitive depiction of male-male desire. This is perhaps because Nirala, an admirer of Shelley and Keats, had a large measure of the "negative capability" requisite to entering into feelings he did not share.

THE AMBIGUITY OF DESIRE IN LITERATURE

Yet, even Ugra, a much lesser writer, finds himself repeatedly drawn towards ambivalence by tropes already laden with a larger and older cultural ambivalence towards eroticism. Here, I would revert to the debate around *Chocolate*, and note that Ugra's opponents — who claimed that literature is inherently more ambivalent than political pamphlets — had a point: metaphoric language is inherently unstable. For instance, in "Chocolate," the boy Ramesh throws an ink bottle at his lover, Dinkar. Dinkar gets soaked in "blue-black" ink, and his kisses stain Ramesh's face as well. Ugra's metaphoric language captures the mixed meanings of this moment: "As if he had played Holi, he was drenched from head to foot." Holi, a modern Hindu festival descended from the ancient spring festival dedicated to Kama, God of love and desire, is traditionally a Saturnalian festival when all desires, especially taboo sexual ones, may be expressed.[99] Revelers throw colored water on one another; getting soaked in color typifies the idiomatic *rang*, or color, of erotic and mystical pleasure. In devotional poetry from the medieval period onwards, this metaphorical color is blue-black, the color of Krishna's complexion, in which his friends, the milkmen and married milkmaids of Braj, get dyed when they play Holi with him. Mystic poets long to be immersed in this blue-black color.

On the other hand, the blue-black ink covering Dinkar and Ramesh also evokes the traditional Indian punishment of blackening wrongdoers' faces and parading them in public. Idiomatically, one who does something shameful is referred to as having blackened his face, *munh kala kiya*, and two people who conduct an illicit affair are said to have blackened their faces with one another. Appropriately, Dinkar reacts to Ramesh's punitive yet intimate gesture with mixed emotions, "overcome with humiliation, anger, shame and desire all at once."

Like the blue-black color on the lovers' faces, the meanings of Ugra's stories refuse singularity; in 2007, as in 1927, fictional and even nonfictional depictions of same-sex eroticism exceed the intentional judgments of authors and critics, signifying differently for different readers, contexts, and times. This translation, then, constitutes yet another blue-black text, its colored ink both covering and uncovering its face.

NOTES

1. I refer to the author throughout as Ugra; this is the way he was and is referred to in the Hindi literary world. *Chocolate* was first published by Mahadev Prasad Seth, at Bisvin Sadi Pustakalaya (Twentieth Century Library), in October 1927, and went into a second edition in December 1927. Seth was the editor of *Matvala*, and the press belonged to him. A third edition appeared in 1953 from Tandon Brothers, Calcutta.

2. It is worth noting, though, that classical Persian and Sanskrit have a common ancestry in a lost Indo-European language, and thus many words are related at the root, a relationship that often transfers to modern languages derived from Persian and Sanskrit.

3. In Sanskrit poetics, which was further developed by medieval and modern literary critics in Sanskrit-based languages, all literature evokes one or more of nine *rasas* (literally "juices," and metaphorically, emotions such as anger, fear, love, and so on).

4. Ashtavakra is a sage, renowned for his knowledge, who appears in many ancient texts, including the *Mahabharata*. The radically nondualist Vedanta text, *Ashtavakra Gita*, is named after him. He also makes cameo appearances in fourteenth-century Bengali devotional texts, such as the *Krittivasa Ramayana*, in which he blesses the infant Bhagiratha, who is miraculously born from the intercourse of two women. The name Ashtavakra means "bent in eight places" and refers to the sage's disabled body, which plays a significant role in narratives about him. For more on the sage, see my essay "Disability as Opportunity: Sage Ashtavakra Mentors Bhagiratha, the Disabled Child of Two Mothers," in

Ruth Vanita, *Gandhi's Tiger and Sita's Smile: Essays on Gender, Sexuality and Culture* (New Delhi: Yoda Press, 2005), 236–50. "*Aayen, Baayen, Saayen*" refers to one who moves in all directions simultaneously, that is, to a person who behaves in an eccentric and unpredictable manner and talks nonsense.

5. Well-known injunction from the *Brihadaranyaka Upanishad*, meaning, "Lead me from the unreal to the real."

6. Quoted in Chaturvedi's editorial, "*Ghasleti Sahitya,*" *Vishal Bharat*, February 1929, 285.

7. Ibid., 286.

8. *Vishal Bharat*, April 1929, 559.

9. Following the violence at Chauri Chaura in 1922, Gandhi called off the civil disobedience movement and embarked on a constructive program intended to combat untouchability and other forms of oppression, as well as to build a self-reliant Indian economy.

10. Quoted in editorial in *Vishal Bharat*, July–August 1929.

11. Saraswati is the name of a river mentioned in the Vedas, and also of the Goddess of wisdom, learning and the arts, mentioned in the Vedas and still widely worshiped today.

12. *Chand*, May 1929, 83.

13. Suman [Shri Ramnathlal], "*Chocolate aur Paalat,*" *Matvala*, August 23, 1924, 6–7.

14. The first edition was published in October and the second in December 1927. Ratnakar Pandey, in *Ugra aur Unka Sahitya* (Varanasi: Nagaripracharini Sabha, 1969), 257–58, hyperbolically claims that "edition upon edition" sold out.

15. Nirala [Suryakanta Tripathi], "*Sahitya mein Propaganda,*" editorial in *Sudha*, September 1933, reproduced in *Nirala Rachanavali* [Collected Works], ed. Nandkishor Naval (New Delhi: Rajkamal Prakashan, 1983), 6:405–8. Nirala pursued the same theme in a 1934 essay, "*Samalochana ya Propaganda?*" *Nirala Rachanavali*, 5:376–83. In this essay, he noted that he was the author of the motto for *Matvala* (381).

16. Nirala [Suryakanta Tripathi]. "*Sahitya ki Navin Pragati Par,*" *Sahitya Samalochak* (May–July 1928), reproduced in *Nirala Rachanavali*, 5:223–32, 224. These inventions may be Chaturvedi's greatest claim to fame, as both names stuck.

17. Nirala [Suryakanta Tripathi]. "*Sahitya mein Samalochana*" (1934), in *Nirala Rachanavali* 5:513–15.

18. Quoted in Pandey, *Ugra aur Unka Sahitya*, 266–67.

19. Anthony Comstock (1844–1915) was a politician dedicated to state enforcement of puritan morality. He founded the Society for the Suppression of Vice, which unsuccessfully tried to have *The Well of Loneliness* banned in the

United States. In 1873, he succeeded in getting Congress to pass the Comstock Law, which made it illegal to transport "obscene, lewd or lascivious material" and methods of or information about birth control. He zealously enforced censorship of materials he considered pornographic, ranging from Bernard Shaw's plays to anatomy textbooks and sex education manuals.

20. Saleem Kidwai, "Firaq Gorakhpuri: Poet versus Critic," in Ruth Vanita and Saleem Kidwai, ed., *Same-Sex Love in India: Readings in Literature and History* (New York: St. Martin's Press, 2000), 264–66.

21. Sitaram Das, "*Bhumika*," in Ugra [Pandey Bechan Sharma], *Chocolate* (Calcutta: Bisvin Sadi Pustakalaya, December 1927), ix–xiv.

22. For more on Gandhi's views on male homosexuality, see Vanita and Kidwai, *Same-Sex Love in India*, 253–56.

23. Quoted in Mohansingh Sengar, "*Ek Sahityik Anarth*," in *Chocolate* (Calcutta: Tandon Brothers, 1953), 1–3, quote on p. 1.

24. Banarasidass Chaturvedi, "*Gandhiji Bapu ke Rup Mein*," *Hindustan*, Gandhi Jayanti issue, October 2, 1951.

25. Quoted in Sengar, "*Ek Sahityik Anarth*," 2.

26. Chaturvedi's letter to Sengar, July 23, 1952, reproduced in Ugra, *Chocolate* (Calcutta: Tandon Brothers, 1953), 12.

27. Despite Nirala's denial that this was the reason for Ugra's quitting the Hindi literary world, Ugra himself cited this as the reason. See Ugra [Pandey Bechan Sharma], *Apni Khabar* (1960; Delhi: Rajkamal, 1984), 105.

28. Chandragupt Vidyalankar, "*Ghaslet-Sahitya*," *Vishal Bharat*, September 1929, 357–64, quote on p. 357.

29. Pandey Bechan Sharma "Ugra," *About Me*, translated and with an introduction by Ruth Vanita (New Delhi: Penguin, 2007). All further citations refer to this translation.

30. Ugra, *About Me*, 19.

31. Nirala, *Nirala Rachanavali*, 5:482–83.

32. Compare Yeats's lines, "Love has pitched his mansion in / The place of excrement / And nothing can be whole or sole / That has not been rent." *Ayoni*, or nonvaginal sexual intercourse, is prohibited in ancient Hindu law books, but paradoxically, many heroes and deities are born of *ayoni* intercourse. For an analysis of the way Hindu sacred narrative texts creatively flout the proscription of *ayoni* sex, see Ruth Vanita, *Love's Rite: Same-Sex Marriage in India and the West* (New York: Palgrave, 2005), especially the introduction and chapter 6.

33. The term "chocolate" is an erotic trope in other cultures; cf. the Cuban gay film *Strawberries and Chocolate* (1993), the American gay film *Better than Chocolate* (1999), and the American film *Chocolat* (2000), which depicts a battle between puritanical and hedonistic forces in a village.

34. Interestingly, as I write, some parents in the United States are demand-

ing that a novel titled *The Chocolate Wars*, which deals explicitly with sexual matters, be banned from school syllabi and libraries.

35. Under Soviet influence, the Indian government did try to eradicate Indian taste for imported consumer items, such as Coca-Cola. These attempts only heightened the demand for smuggled goods.

36. Thanks to Gunjan Sharma of TARSHI for our conversation and for her follow-up email of February 4, 2008.

37. See Vanita and Kidwai, *Same-Sex Love in India*, especially the Preface and "Introduction to Modern Indian Materials."

38. For the purification campaign in Urdu literature, see Vanita and Kidwai, *Same-Sex Love in India*, 200–201, 220; and Frances Pritchett, *Nets of Awareness: Urdu Poetry and its Critics* (Karachi: Oxford University Press, 1995).

39. See Ruth Vanita, "'Married among Their Companions': Female Homoerotic Relations in Nineteenth-Century Urdu *Rekhti* Poetry in India," *Journal of Women's History* 16, no. 1 (spring 2004); and Vanita, *Love's Rite*, chap. 8.

40. See my essay, "Pleasure or Moral Purpose: Conflict and Anxiety in Modern Hindi Translations of the *Kamasutra*," in Vanita, *Gandhi's Tiger and Sita's Smile*, 268–89.

41. Hakim Mohammad Yusuf Hasan, *Do Shiza*, 3rd ed. (Lahore: n.p., 1934). For an English translation, see Vanita and Kidwai, *Same-Sex Love in India*, 260–63.

42. Ugra, *About Me*, 96. As a schoolboy, however, Ugra disliked this puritanical headmaster and mimicked him in public.

43. Ashis Nandy was the first to analyze this phenomenon in *The Intimate Enemy: Loss and Recovery of Self under Colonialism* (Delhi: Oxford University Press, 1988). See also Mrinalini Sinha, *Colonial Masculinity: The "Manly Englishman" and the "Effeminate Bengali" in the Late Nineteenth Century* (Manchester: Manchester University Press, 1995).

44. See Veena Talwar Oldenburg, "Lifestyle as Resistance: The Case of the Courtesans of Lucknow," in *Lucknow: Memories of a City*, ed. Violette Graff (Oxford: Oxford University Press, 1997), 136; Saleem Kidwai, "The Singing Ladies Find a Voice," *Seminar*, Special Issue "Celebrating Women," no. 540 (August 2004); Davesh Soneji, "Living History, Performing Memory: Devadasi Women in Telugu-Speaking South India," *Dance Research Journal* 36, no. 2 (2005): 30–49.

45. For an account of this trajectory, see Saleem Kidwai, trans., *Song Sung True: A Memoir by Malka Pukhraj* (New Delhi: Kali for Women, 2002).

46. Charu Gupta describes these purification campaigns among Hindus, including campaigns to remove Islamic influences from Hindu life, but omits campaigns among Muslims to remove Hindu influence from Muslim life. See her *Sexuality, Obscenity, Community: Women, Muslims, and the Hindu Public in*

Colonial India (New Delhi: Permanent Black, 2001). See also Shohini Ghosh's film on the Calcutta sex workers' union, *Tales of the Night Fairies*.

47. Michel Foucault, *The History of Sexuality: An Introduction*, vol. 1, trans. Robert Hurley (New York: Random House, 1978); David M. Halperin, *One Hundred Years of Homosexuality* (New York: Routledge, 1990). For an opposing view with regard to European texts, see John Boswell, "Revolutions, Universals, and Sexual Categories," in *Hidden from History: Reclaiming the Gay and Lesbian Past*, ed. Martin Bauml Duberman, Martha Vicinus and George Chauncey (New York: Meridian, 1989), 17–36. For Indian texts, see Michael J. Sweet and Leonard Zwilling, "The First Medicalization: The Taxonomy and Etiology of Queers in Classical Indian Medicine," *Journal of the History of Sexuality* 3, no. 4 (1993): 590–607; "'Like a City Ablaze': The Third Sex and the Creation of Sexuality in Jain Religious Literature," *Journal of the History of Sexuality* 6, no. 3 (1996): 359–84; and Vanita and Kidwai, *Same-Sex Love in India*, xx–xxi; see also my essay, "A Rose by Any Other Name: The Sexuality Terminology Debates," in Vanita, *Gandhi's Tiger and Sita's Smile*, 60–69.

48. Saleem Kidwai, "Introduction: Medieval Materials in the Perso-Urdu Tradition," in Vanita and Kidwai, *Same-Sex Love in India*, 107–25.

49. Thanks to Archana Varma for pointing me to the source of this phrase.

50. Vanita and Kidwai, "Introduction: Modern Indian Materials," in Vanita and Kidwai, *Same-Sex Love in India*, 191–217.

51. See "Dargah Quli Khan: Portrait of a City," translated from Persian by Saleem Kidwai, in Vanita and Kidwai, *Same-Sex Love in India*, 175–83.

52. *Matvala*, April 18, 1925, 390.

53. Letter from Shivpujan, undated, in Ugra [Pandey Bechan Sharma], *File aur Profile* (Delhi: Ranjit Publishers, 1967), 382–84, quotations on pp. 383 and 384. The word for kiss is *chumban* and is enclosed in single quote marks.

54. Letter from Shrikrishnadutt Paliwal, June 27, 1928, in Ugra, *File aur Profile*, 403–5, quotation on p. 403, emphasis in the original.

55. John Boswell, *Christianity, Social Tolerance and Homosexuality: Gay People in Western Europe from the Beginning of the Christian Era to the Fourteenth Century* (Chicago: University of Chicago Press, 1980), 28–29.

56. Contrast, for example, the Hindi movie *Page 3* (2004), directed by Madhur Bhandarkar, which, very much like Ugra's *Phagun ke Din Char*, is a Jeremiad against the upper class and film worlds of Bombay as irredeemably corrupt and vicious. The film climaxes in a scene of adult men molesting boy children. As opposed to Ugra's boys, who are in their teens, the boys in the film appear to be between the ages of five and nine.

57. Liberal nationalists and feminists fought for decades to raise the age of consent. In 1891, following the death of ten-year-old Phulmoni Das from sexual injuries caused by intercourse with her thirtyfive-year-old husband, the

British government raised the age for girls to consent to consummation of marriage from ten to twelve. The ensuing bitter controversy split the Indian National Congress, as eminent leader Bal Gangadhar Tilak opposed it as contrary to Indian tradition. In 1929, the Child Marriage Restraint Act raised the age of consent to fourteen for girls and eighteen for boys. Following both legislations, the legislature warned the executive not to implement the law rigorously, and marriages well under the age of consent continued to occur. In princely states, like Mysore, where the age of marriage was eight for girls, there were many more prosecutions than in British India. See Janaki Nair, *Women and Law in Colonial India: A Social History* (New Delhi: Kali for Women, 1996).

58. For an account of the way this law has been used, see Suparna Bhaskaran, "The Politics of Penetration: Section 377 of the Indian Penal Code," in *Queering India: Same-Sex Love and Eroticism in Indian Culture and Society*, ed. Ruth Vanita (New York: Routledge, 2002), 18–29.

59. On August 11, 1992, AIDS Bhedbhav Virodhi Andolan (AIDS Antidiscrimination Movement), known as ABVA, who had published the pathbreaking report *Less Than Gay* (New Delhi: ABVA, 1991), held the first-ever protest in India condemning police use of Section 377. In March 1994, after authorities at Tihar Jail, Delhi, citing Section 377, refused to make condoms available to prisoners, ABVA filed a public-interest petition in the Delhi high court, asking for repeal of Section 377 on the grounds that it violates constitutional rights to life, liberty, and nondiscrimination, and obstructs AIDS prevention. The petition came up for hearing in March 2001 and was dismissed without arguments, because ABVA failed to appear. In December 2001, Naz Foundation (India) Trust, an anti-AIDS organization, and Lawyers Collective (whose HIV-AIDS unit was set up in 1998) jointly filed a petition in the Delhi high court, asking that Section 377 be interpreted to apply only to sexual assault on children. In September 2004, the court dismissed the petition on the grounds that since the petitioners were not being prosecuted under Section 377, they had no cause of action against it. This decision was appealed to the Supreme Court, which, in 2005, instructed the Delhi high court to admit and hear the case. For more details, see Ruth Vanita, "India Considers Abolishing Sodomy Laws," in *Great Events from History: GLBT Events 1848-2006*, ed. Lillian Faderman et al. (Pasadena, Calif.: Salem Press, 2006).

60. See Vanita, *Love's Rite*, for accounts of many such female couples who either marry, with some family support, or are forcibly separated and even driven to suicide. See also Ruth Vanita, "'What the Heart Says': Same-Sex Unions in the Context of Globalized Homophobia and Globalized Gay Rights," in *India in the Age of Globalization: Contemporary Discourses and Texts*, ed. Tapan Basu et al. (New Delhi: Pearson, forthcoming 2009).

61. For a discussion of the controversy around the use of Western terms such as *lesbian* and *gay* in India, see my introduction in Vanita, *Queering India*.

62. For an account of these debates today, see Vanita, *Love's Rite*, esp. chap. 10.

63. See Geeta Patel, "On Fire: Sexuality and Its Incitements," 222–33, and Monica Bachmann, "After the Fire," both in Vanita, *Queering India*, 234–44.

64. Parsi theater, an important influence on modern India's theatrical and cinematic traditions, was popular from the 1850s to the 1950s, not only in India but in surrounding countries as well. Unlike Ramlila and other traditional religious dramas, which were normally staged in the open air or under makeshift roofing, Parsi theater used the European proscenium and catered to a cosmopolitan urban audience. Plays were acted in urban Gujarati, Hindi, and Urdu.

65. For an analysis of males playing female roles in Parsi theater, see Kathryn Hansen, "A Different Desire, a Different Femininity: Theatrical Transvestism in the Parsi, Gujarati and Marathi Theaters, 1850–1940," in Vanita, *Queering India*, 163–80.

66. See Shitikanth Mishra, *"Ugra: Vyaktitva evam Krititva ki Jhalkiyan,"* in *Pandey Bechan Sharma 'Ugra,'* ed. Sudhakar Pandey (Varanasi: Nagaripracharini Sabha, 2001), 165–70, quote on p. 166.

67. In a 1964 interview by S. Lakshman Shastri, Ugra boasts that he had, in the course of his life, spent Rs. 50,000 on horse races, and the same amount on intoxicants. He also instructs the interviewer to bring a bottle of liquor with him on his next visit.

68. See Ugra, *About Me*, and also Sitaram Dwivedi, *"Ugraji, Matvala aur Mahadevprasad Seth,"* in Pandey, *Pandey Bechan Sharma 'Ugra,'* 115–17.

69. Kalikaprasad Dixit, *"Ram Ram Kehnewala Ugraji ka Kutta,"* in Pandey, *Pandey Bechan Sharma 'Ugra,'* 120.

70. See Pandey, *Pandey Bechan Sharma 'Ugra,'* esp. 108 and 114. For the vow of celibacy, see Veniram Tripathi, *"Chand Tasveeren,"* in the same book, 124. In the same book, too, Vishnu Prabhakar, *"Ugraji: Meri Drishti Mein,"* reports that Ugra told him that many men hesitated to invite him to their homes because of their young daughters and daughters-in-law (31).

71. Bhavadev Pandey, *Pandey Bechan Sharma 'Ugra,' Bharatiya Sahitya ke Nirmata* (New Delhi: Sahitya Akademi, 2001), 66.

72. Mohanlal Ratnakar, *Pandey Bechan Sharma Ugra Kahanikar, Upanyaskar* (Delhi: Rishabhcharan Jain and Sons, 1974), 69. Among others who take the same view are Madhu Dhar, *Ugra ka Katha Sahitya* (Delhi: Rajpal and Sons, 1977); and Bhavadev Pandey, *Pandey Bechan Sharma 'Ugra.'*

73. Mohanlal Tiwari, "Ugraji ki Rachana ka Shastriya Paksh" [The Aesthetic Dimension of Ugra's Composition], in Sudhakar Pandey, *Pandey Bechan Sharma 'Ugra,'* 176–77.

74. "*Adarsh Upanyas,*" *Sahitya Sandesh*, August 1940, 450, 452.

75. The word translated as "intense" is *ugra*, the author's own pen name.

76. The word translated here and in the previous line as "pleasure" is *bhog*, which can also mean sexual intercourse.

77. These two lines are heavily alliterative — eleven of the fourteen words begin with the letter *ka*.

78. Literally, a member of the *sant sampradaya*.

79. This is a back-handed compliment — Ugra uses idiomatic Sanskrit and Hindi phrases, both of which strongly suggest hypocritical asceticism like that of the crane, which appears to be immersed in meditation until a fish comes within its reach.

80. This translation is from Ugra [Pandey Bechan Sharma], *Phagun ke Din Char* (Delhi: Ranjit Publishers, 1960), 83–84.

81. *Kamasutram* (1911; Bombay: Venkateswara Steam Press, 1995), 15.

82. For a detailed analysis see Ruth Vanita, "Pleasure or Moral Purpose: Conflict and Anxiety in Modern Hindi Translations of the *Kamasutra,*" in Vanita, *Gandhi's Tiger and Sita's Smile*.

83. On the overlap between friendship, love, and marriage in ancient and medieval Hindu texts, see Vanita and Kidwai, *Same-Sex Love in India*, 2–12, 90–93; and Vanita, *Love's Rite*, esp. chap. 6, "A Second Self: Traditions of Romantic Friendship."

84. Ugra, *Phagun ke Din Char*, 84–85.

85. See Ugra, *About Me*, 62–63. For *ranginmijaaz* as a term for homoerotic inclination, see Vanita and Kidwai, *Same-Sex Love in India*, 192.

86. See Vanita and Kidwai, *Same-Sex Love in India*, 191–94, 210, 220–21; Vanita, *Love's Rite*, 185, 203–4; 206–7, 222.

87. *Outlook* (India), September 11, 1996, in a cover story entitled "Sex in the 90s: Uneasy Revolution," reported that a reader survey, conducted in eight cities, found that Lucknow scored the highest both in reader experience and acceptance of homosexuality, with 34 percent of respondents from Lucknow admitting to the experience and 46 percent considering it normal. In January 2006, police entrapped and arrested four gay men in Lucknow after monitoring their activities on the Internet. LGBT and human-rights organizations, both national and international, protested the arrests. The men were subsequently released on bail, and the case serves as evidence in the lawsuit against Section 377, proving that the antisodomy provision is not, as government officials often claim it is, used only against child molesters. For more details of the Lucknow arrests, see Ruth Vanita, "What the Heart Says: Same-Sex Unions in the Context of Globalized Homophobia and Globalized Gay Rights," in Basu et al., ed., *India in the Age of Globalization*.

88. For an entertaining analysis of the contradictions permeating the lives

of modern Indian denouncers of Westernization, see Nirala's essay, "*Samajik Paradhinta*," in *Nirala Rachanavali*, 6:133–38.

89. For more on *The Well* and Indian readers, see my essay, "Tragic Love and the Ungendered Heart: Reading *The Well of Loneliness* in India and the West," in Vanita, *Gandhi's Tiger and Sita's Smile*, 136–53.

90. Ramachandra Guha, "The Independent Journal of Opinion," *Seminar* 481 (September 1999). www.india-seminar.com/1999/481/481%20guha.htm. See also Amartya Sen, "Tagore and His India," *New York Review of Books*, June 26, 1997. http://nobelprize.org/literature/articles/sen/.

91. Sabyasachi Bhattacharya, ed., *The Mahatma and the Poet: Letters and Debates between Gandhi and Tagore 1915–1941* (New Delhi: National Book Trust, 1997), 64. Page numbers for all citations from Tagore's and Gandhi's writings refer to this edition.

92. "*Sahitya ki Samtal Bhumi*" (1926), in *Nirala Rachanavali*, 5:156. See also "*Saundarya Darshan aur Kavi Kaushal*" (1928), ibid., 215–23.

93. Nirala [Suryakant Tripathi], "*Vyapak Sahitya*" (1930), in *Nirala Rachanavali*, 5:455–57.

94. Nirala [Suryakant Tripathi], "*Navin Sahitya aur Prachin Vichar*" (1929), in *Nirala Rachanavali*, 5:441.

95. Nirala [Suryakant Tripathi], "*Bangal ke Vaishnav Kaviyon ka Shringar Varnana*" (1928), in *Nirala Rachanavali* 5:246–63.

96. See Nirala [Suryakant Tripathi], *Nirala Rachanavali*, 4:21–81. For a translation of relevant portions of this novelette, see Vanita and Kidwai, *Same-Sex Love in India*, 270–73. Page numbers in the text refer to this translation.

97. Nirala [Suryakant Tripathi], dedication to *Kulli Bhaat*, in *Nirala Rachanavali*, 4:19.

98. One may compare the fears often expressed by opponents of same-sex marriage, to the effect that people may start demanding the right to marry their pets.

99. This tradition continues today. For example, in the 1981 Hindi film *Silsila* (Sequence), the protagonist, a married man having an affair with a married woman, consumes bhang, an intoxicant traditionally imbibed on Holi, and then sings an erotic song, "*Rang Barse*" (Color Showers), while dancing with and throwing color on her, thus revealing their relationship. The song is now among the most popular Holi songs, continually replayed on television during the festival.

Apriyasya cha satyasya shrota vakta durlabhaha.

It is hard to find a speaker of or a listener to unpleasant truths.

ALL THE NAMES AND CHARACTERS IN THIS BOOK ARE
IMAGINARY, AND THE INCIDENTS ARE ALL IMAGINED
POSSIBILITIES. NO GENTLEMAN (?) SHOULD LOOK
FOR HIS NAME OR LIFE HERE.

If relations with a woman not one's wife, relations with a prostitute, drinking alcohol, and gambling are social sins, then unnatural acts or following the path of chocolate is a great sin. If society preaches against and openly debates the former sins, why should this sin not be preached against and criticized?

If this is not done, one day our society, too, will become like that land where beautiful boys are kept as mistresses, and are the prey of men's desires.

If this happens in India, our culture and civilization will be totally destroyed, which is not permissible.

UGRA

FOREWORD

"I have nothing to sell, I am not mad, I have no fears."

I say to the puppet-masters of government—and to each of the fibers that make up the strings they wield; I say to the wise men in society—and to each of their auspicious thoughts; I say to the beautiful playthings of the country—and to their tender childish intellects; listen to my words, let me speak!

I say to the educational institutions of society; to the "weak" men whose *duty* it is to be the gods of child welfare institutions; I say to the carefully disguised and hidden ones who live in the alleys and streets of every city, who dive deep to swallow fish, who eat seventy mice themselves and then advise others to go on pilgrimage[1]; I say to the gentlemen who invoke ideals and customs, who cover the truth with a cloak of deception, who conceal their own voices and take on a tone of armored seriousness; listen to my words, let me speak!

Is there any mother's son who, having looked at our present-day society from top to bottom with alert eyes, can put his hand on his heart, raise up his head, emboldened by the light of truth, and dare say to the poor author of this book: "Whatever you have written is wrong. There are no such loathsome, horrifying and black pictures in society!" If there is any such, let him come forward, twist my ears, slap my small

1. The proverb, "Having eaten seventy mice, the cat goes on Haj [pilgrimage to Mecca]," refers to the hypocrisy of wrongdoers who pretend to be pious.

face, and settle my wits once for all. I will welcome that great man's rebukes with a happy heart, I will humbly accept his curses, and change my ways. I speak truly, believe me; I do not need oaths or witnesses.

Ever since I have been old enough to fully observe and assess our present-day society I have been wondering when I would have the opportunity to attract people's attention, in words as clear as possible, to this hellish vice directed against beautiful boys of tender years. Finally, I got the opportunity, and I used it as I wished. My first story, entitled "Chocolate," against what society calls "boy-chasing" and what I call "the path of chocolate," was published on May 31, 1924, in Calcutta's famous troublemaking newspaper *Matvala*.[2] I well remember that before I wrote the story I expressed my desire to the editor of a well-known Hindi newspaper and a very famous novelist, and asked those respected gentlemen: "What is your advice? Should something be written on this subject or not? If not, why not?" Mr. Editor was speechless at first! Perhaps he had never imagined that it would ever be necessary to say or hear anything about a subject like chocolate. Perhaps he was afraid that this overeager writer might dare write something in his newspaper. He replied in a roundabout manner and then assumed a solemn expression. The meaning of his reply was both "yes" and "no." Now it was the turn of Mr. Novelist. At first, looking at me with innocent eyes, he burst out laughing, "Ha ha ha ha ha!" Then he said, "Ugraji, what you say is absolutely true, but, brother, it's no easy job to write or read about this topic. Not everybody can speak such an unpleasant truth and still face society. At least, I cannot say a word on this topic." I thought to myself, Very well. It is I who will take this *risk*. I will play this unpleasant part in an unpleasant play.

The story "Chocolate" was published in *Matvala*. The story shrouded all the newspapers in a pall of silence, but aroused a storm among readers. Not one or two but sheaves and sheaves of letters, both of praise and blame, began to come to the editor of *Matvala* and to the author of the story. Lines of worry appeared on the brows of the grave; frivolous laughter colored the cheeks of the shallow. In one day, spoken but once, the word "chocolate" spread to every corner of the Hindi

2. *Laundebaazi* and *chocolate panthi*, respectively.

world! The letters kept coming, the storms kept arising, the frowns of disapproval kept spreading, hatred kept coming before me and pulling hateful faces to shake my resolution, and I kept writing more stories. After "Chocolate," at intervals of several months, I wrote four more stories, "Kept Boy," "We Are in Love with Lucknow," "Waist Curved Like a She-Cobra," and "Discussing Chocolate." While I was writing the last story, I had to go to Bombay. Then, a warrant was issued against me under 124A; I was prosecuted for my editorship of the victory issue of *Swadesh*, and was thrown into the womb of jail for nine months.[3]

When I emerged from jail, many of my friends very affectionately whispered in my ears: "Look, Ugra, you have developed a very bad reputation as a result of those stories on chocolate that you wrote in *Matvala*. People everywhere are criticizing you, calling you 'frivolous,' 'boy [*launda*],' 'chocolate,' and who knows what else. Brother, don't write any more such stories! Enough of this topic! To hell with chocolate and its discussion. When the whole society prefers to keep quiet about this subject, why are you so intent on playing with fire?" My friends were right in what they said. But my desire to bring this issue to light did not diminish. I determined in my heart that whatever happened, I would not give up the subject without creating an uproar about it. In fulfillment of that resolution, I wrote three more stories; I have now completed this chocolate-collection, and have put it before society. I truly believe in my heart that, utilizing my status as a completely negligible person in society, it is my duty to start a movement around this issue. I am doing this as a duty, and I am ready to taste the fruits of this act.

A few other voices have also been heard here and there, after my stories against these vile transactions were published. I heard that

3. The special issue Ugra edited was deemed seditious by the British government, under section 124A of the Indian Penal Code, 1860: "Whoever, by words, either spoken or written, or by signs, or by visible representation, or otherwise, brings or attempts to bring into hatred or contempt, or excites or attempts to excite disaffection towards the Government established by law shall be punished with [imprisonment for life], to which fine may be added, or with imprisonment which may extend to three years, to which fine may be added, or with fine."

some male or female writer had informed Mahatma Gandhi about these sins, which can be found, along with Mahatmaji's opinion, if one searches through the files of *Hindi Navajivan* or *Young India* of 1926. The *Surya* from Banaras also, which appeared every other day, perhaps in 1926 itself, serially published a number of essays entitled "Chocolate-followers." And, very recently, an essay on the theme also appeared in the famous *Pratap* of Kanpur, which the highly competent and famous editor published with "much embarrassment." No doubt there is a difference between the style and narrative technique of these essays and my stories. These essays are written in as restrained a style as possible, and truth is concealed under many layers of cultured language. The sharp quinine of truth has been coated in sugar so that society can swallow it easily. I have not done this in my stories — partly due to my extreme habits of writing and partly due to my love for the naked truth.[4] My stories are not *sugarcoated quinine* but pure, bitter quinine or cinchona. Even the worst patient will sit up and take notice on drinking this mixture, and will look at me and make a face. There is no doubt about this. I know it well.

If there is any art in depicting truth exactly as it is, then there is art in my stories too. But if not, if art is not always pure truth, then these blazing stories of mine are devoid of art. I do not know how to create such art nor do I try to know such art.

If any reader of *Chocolate* is kind enough to give some thought to the viciousness of the topic and the difficulties the writer faced when making it the theme of fiction, I am sure he will feel some sympathy for me even in the midst of his anger. That's all I desire!

Read it — let the elders and great ones in society read this hellish creation of Ugra, not to enjoy the stories or art, not to witness the flights of my talent, but to secure the brightness of their own children's future. To protect them from the demons who assume many different forms in society. To safeguard their energy and virginity.[5] To keep them far from animality and close to humanity.

4. The word translated as "extreme" is *ugra*.
5. The word used is *brahmacharya*. This term refers to the state of pre-

Read it—let our young friends standing on the threshold of life definitely read this black composition of mine; and, having read it, let them refrain from letting the hateful shadow of their hearts fall on the tender heart of any companion or friend of theirs. Let them hesitate to paint his face with the ink of desire. Let them not spread smoke in the chambers of their hearts or set fire to an innocent friend's home.

Read it—let beautiful children, the small, flowerlike playthings of the country, also read these lines of mine, and, from the start, tremble for fear of the conspiracies, the temptations, the vices of those followers of the path of chocolate. Viewing these demonic pictures, let them learn to recognize those demons and learn to protect their own flowering pink cheeks from those attacks, to keep safe the redness of their petal-like lips, and to consider the purity of their hearts more important than the worthless lures and baits they are offered.

I have faults, and no doubt my writings, too, are faulty. But readers should read any work with the immortal lines of the poet in mind:

The creator made the universe
Moving and unmoving, full of merits and faults,
Like the swan, the good person drinks the milk,
And avoids the defects.[6]

Enough: I have said what I had to.

Pandey Bechan Sharma "Ugra"

Matvala Mandal,
Calcutta

---

marital celibacy traditionally considered appropriate to the first twenty-five years of life dedicated to study, and also refers to the vow of celibacy taken by ascetics.

6. Famous verse from Tulsidas's *Ramcharitmanas*. The reference is to the belief that swans are able to filter out and drink the milk from a mixture of milk and water. The word translated as "defect" is *vikar*, literally, "crooked," which in modern Hindi also comes to mean "perversion."

CHOCOLATE

1.

"Oh how I suffer, love has made me its prey.
Never has my heart been so wounded as today."[1]
Softly reciting this verse in a pathetic tone, my friend Babu Dinkar Prasad, B.A., flopped on to a chair, like an intoxicated person.[2] I silently wondered what had happened. Why was he so languorous today? I asked, "Are you all right? You seem like a Majnun today."[3]

Dinkar Babu sighed deeply once more, and said,
"I had no acquaintance with grief, no knowledge of sorrow.
Those were happy days before I fell in love."

A verse, a sigh, and then a full stop! Somewhat annoyed, I remarked to my other friend, Manohar Chandra, who was also sitting there, "Do you see this, Mannu? Today he's inaugurated a poetry recital. He's

This story, the first of Ugra's eight stories on the subject of homosexuality, was first published on May 31, 1924, in *Matvala*. In 1927, it appeared as the title story in the collection of the same name.

1. The verses Dinkar recites are all Urdu *shers*, or verse couplets.

2. The word translated as "intoxicated person" is *matvala*. This epithet provocatively identifies Dinkar with the newspaper and its readers.

3. Majnun is the hero of the Persian Laila-Majnun romance, widely rewritten in India. His name is now idiomatic for a love-struck man.

started keeping secrets even from us. I wonder who's enchanted him."[4]

Manohar Chandra was also fed up with Dinkar Prasad's riddles. It was surprising that he had kept quiet so long, because Manohar was a chatterbox. Now he said, "Babu Dinkar Prasad is a being from another planet. His idea is:

'I kissed the eyebrow that I found so beautiful

I felt as if a sword had struck my lips.'"[5]

"Oh. Such a beautiful Banarasi poem! Whose is it, buddy? Kissing the eyebrow, a sword on the lips. Eyebrows compared to a sword striking the lips! Wow!"

"Has your fine lady, Urdu, been defeated by such a simple simile?" said Manohar, smiling. "Hear another one:

'I asked, Why have you put collyrium in your eyes?

She laughed and said, A knife is sharpened on a stone.'"

Dinkar: "Excellent. Eyes and a knife, collyrium and a stone. It's really very good."

When Dinkar praised the verse so highly, I said to Manohar, "Recite the one about the noose. Dinkar Babu will enjoy it very much."

"Yes, yes! Listen, Dinkar Babu!" said Manohar, and began:

"Ever since I fell into the noose of your locks,

O God! I wander, lost, as if in a maze.

I look at you through half-closed eyes,

O God! neither am I drugged nor am I able to sleep.

Alas, caught in the rope of your love,

Kings, thieves, and wise men all wait for slaughter.

'I am renouncing the world in your alley,'

So saying to my companions, I came here today."

I clearly remember what happened next. Manohar had not quite finished reciting the poem when someone called out from the door: "Dinkar Babu!"

4. Literally, what piece of the moon (that is, what beautiful person) he has seen.

5. Manohar's verses are all in Banarasi Hindi. This couplet and the next are in the style of *chher chhaar*, teasing.

"Yes, yes, it's you! I'm coming."

"Excuse me, brothers. It's urgent. I'll see you tomorrow." So saying, Dinkar Babu leapt towards the door. We saw that a beautiful lad of thirteen or fourteen was waiting for him there!

2.

I asked Manohar, "Who was that boy? Is he a relative of Dinkar?"[6]

"Oh no. He's Dinkar's 'chocolate.'"

"Chocolate?? What do you mean chocolate?"

"Pocketbook."

"Explain what you mean, stop joking! Your chocolates and pocketbooks are Latin and Greek to me."

"It's easier to understand Latin and Greek, brother; to study these chocolates is very difficult. This chocolate disease is spreading in our country faster than plague or cholera. Society sees it all but pretends to be blind. People oppose prostitution, and are angered by widow remarriage, but will not even mention this. Why? Because society is embarrassed. The house is on fire but these *gentlemen* are too ashamed to put it out!"

"Explain a little more. I haven't really understood."

"All right, let me tell you clearly, memorize this definition of chocolate. It's possible you too may have to face it. 'Chocolate' is a name for those innocent, tender, and beautiful boys of our country, whom society's demons push into the mouth of destruction to quench their own desires. Highly respectable people in our society destroy these boys and make them bad charactered.[7] There are many different names for them in different regions. In our United Provinces, people call them

6. Literally, "some brother of Dinkar?," a phrase that suggests he is a cousin, but could also refer to a brother.

7. "Good charactered" and "bad charactered" are very commonly used in Hindi and in Indian English, generally to indicate sexual morality or lack thereof. The Sanskrit/Hindi equivalent, used here, is *dushcharitra* (bad charactered).

'chocolate' and 'pocketbook.'[8] There are also many names for them which cannot be written in civilized language."

"What? Can an educated person like Dinkar Babu fall into such a swamp of sin? Impossible! You must be mistaken, Manohar."

"Mistaken! All right, you talk to him about this subject in a sympathetic way and see what he says. He'll sift through history, finish off the Puranas, and prove to you that love of boys is not unnatural but natural.[9] When I talked to him about it, he told me, on the basis of an English book, that even Socrates was guilty of this offence. He said that Shakespeare too was a slave of some beautiful friend of his. He spoke of Mr. Oscar Wilde as well. If you don't believe me talk to him yourself and see if I'm right."

3.

"Dear Gopal!

"Last evening I discussed 'chocolate' with you. When I returned home I felt that I had not explained the topic to you properly so I am writing this letter today. I would have liked to meet you, but I have to go to Prayag right now for some urgent work.[10]

"I have reflected a lot on this matter. Society is suffering terrible harm because of it. The youth of this country are becoming effeminate. When a boy sees that many people are attracted to one of his companions, he, too, tries to imitate that companion. He starts trying to become a chocolate by using Venolea and then White Rose and then Pears Soap.[11] Instead of studying, boys spend their time trying to look handsome. And once they fall into the trade of beauty their intellect is weakened, their desires are strengthened, and they develop loath-

8. The state later called Uttar Pradesh.

9. Literally, he will do the *kapalkriya* of the *Puranas*. The *Puranas* are medieval devotional story-cycles, dedicated to various Gods and Goddesses. *Kapalkriya* refers to the act of breaking the skull when a corpse is being cremated.

10. Prayag is an older Hindu name for the city of Allahabad.

11. All supposedly help to lighten the complexion.

some habits. Many boys are destroyed because of their guardians' incompetence. Most guardians do not try to reform the secret lives of their sons. It's enough for them if the boys go to school and come back home, and pass at the end of the year or at least get promoted.

"There are all kinds of places in this country where boys can get ruined. Most of the efforts to mislead boys occur at boarding schools, Brahmacharya ashrams, Company[12] Gardens, fairs and festivals. One often hears of teachers being responsible for boys' ruin. There are few schools where five to ten such cases do not come before the headmaster each year. Despite this, people do not bother about reform. There are few students who do not have a handsome friend. Students say their beautiful friends are just friends or relatives. But it is impossible to describe how they behave with these friends and relatives.

"Therefore, Gopu, this bad custom must be put an end to. Otherwise, the present generation in our country will destroy future generations as well. Very soon, bravery, virtue, and humanity will be completely destroyed. Enough—more when we meet.

Your Manohar."

*　　*　　*　　*

A sigh escaped me when I read Manohar's letter. Even fate is opposed to the weak![13] How many ailments afflict enslaved India?

By chance, that very day, at about ten in the morning, Dinkar Babu arrived at my house with his young friend. The boy's face showed that he was intelligent. His bright eyes indicated that if he took the right path he could become a 'beautiful Indian.' To throw such a beautiful flower into the furnace! To put a gift of the Gods at the feet of a donkey!! Dinkar Babu disgusted me. I asked him, "Who is he to you?"

"He—he's my friend, the lawyer Mr. Banwarilal's son."

I said, "That doesn't answer my question. What is he to you?"

12. Company here denotes, like the Company school of painting, the East India Company, which ruled India before the Crown took over in 1858, and established gardens in various cities.

13. Sanskrit idiom, quoted here in Sanskrit.

"He is nothing special to me. I'm his father's friend, so he sometimes comes to study with me. You can consider him my younger brother."

"Fine; please sit down, and I'll bring something to eat."

I deliberately left the two of them alone. As I went into the house I saw that the boy's eyes were lowered in shame. Telling my wife to put some snacks on two plates for the guests, I hid behind the door to watch Dinkar Babu and his 'younger brother.' They were both sitting at the table, somewhat apart from each other.

There was a moment's silence. Then Dinkar said, "Well?"

The boy looked at him and remained silent.

"Where were you yesterday?"

He still kept quiet.

"Answer me. How come you forgot me yesterday? You know I cannot be happy without you for even a moment. I couldn't sleep at night. I kept wondering whether you were angry with me. Oh! How much I love you. Come here!!"

This time, the boy replied, with a mixture of fear and indifference, "What nonsense you talk. If someone hears us, what will they think?"

"Let them think what they like. Does one need anyone's permission to love? I love you. Come here!

'Love is a pain, a fever, a torment.

Shaikh, how can you know what love is?'[14]

Come here, Ramesh!"

"Say whatever you want from there. I won't come any nearer."

"I want to tell you in your ear. It's a secret. Come, I beg you, come!"[15]

"Ugh! No."

"'A fleeting glance of love is the price of this heart.

This bargain is on sale, what are your orders?'"

14. An Urdu couplet. The Shaikh is a conventionally Puritanical figure in Urdu poetry, who opposes love, considering it idolatrous.

15. Literally, "I adjure you by myself," a very common Indian way of compelling someone to do something. It is feared that ignoring such an adjuration may lead to disaster befalling the adjurer.

This time Dinkar Babu sang the verse softly and repeated, "Come, Ramesh."

"What nonsense! This is someone else's house. Say what you have to say. Who else is here to overhear?"

"You won't come. Fine, then I'll come to you. If Mohammad won't go to the mountain, the mountain must come to Mohammad.

'Mir dies a thousand times in an instant.

He has devised a new way to live.'"[16]

As he sang, Dinkar Babu, aflame with desire, drew his chair towards Ramesh.

"Someone will come. Your friend . . ."

Ramesh got up from his chair and stood next to the table. He said, "Please don't ever talk to me in future."[17]

"Why, why, beloved?[18] Why are you angry with me?" said Dinkar, moving towards him.

A bottle of *blue-black* ink stood on the table. Ramesh picked it up and said, "Don't come any closer. Otherwise I will hit you with this. Someone else's house—have you no shame?"

The breeze of anger stirred desire's intoxication. Dinkar became even more excited. Making a move to pounce on the boy, he said, "You are mine. I have a right to you. Why are you angry? Come here."

Seeing him pounce, Ramesh pretended to throw the ink bottle at him, merely intending to frighten him. But look at this!! The bottle remained in his hand, but the cork came off. Dinkar Babu was soaked in ink!! As if he had played Holi, he was drenched from head to foot.

Dinkar was overcome with humiliation, anger, shame, and desire all at once. Ramesh stood stunned by this sudden turn of events. Dinkar

16. This couplet is by Mir Taqi Mir (ca. 1723–1810), generally considered the greatest of all Urdu poets. For more homoerotic verse by him, see Ruth Vanita and Saleem Kidwai, *Same Sex Love in India* (New York: Palgrave, 2000), 184–90.

17. In Hindi, the verb "to talk" can be a euphemism for sexual interaction. The double meaning is similar to that of *conversation* in older English.

18. The word used is *Pyare*. The same word is translated later as "darling."

caught hold of him and began to embrace and kiss him: "Angry with me? With me? Darling, darling!"

* * * *

Just then, I entered the room. Hearing my step, Dinkar released Ramesh. Ramesh's face was also black from contact with his ink-stained face!

I said, "Dinkar Babu, I had just arranged snacks for you but now I will also have to fetch soap, water, and towels. Perhaps I should give you clothes to change into as well. Your love for your 'younger brother' is worth witnessing. Very well, you stay here. I will take Ramesh to his father's house."

4.

After this incident, Dinkar was not to be found anywhere. Six months have passed, but no one has heard anything of him.

Ramesh's father has begun to keep a strict eye on his son's private life. May God protect Ramesh!

KEPT BOY

1.

'Love has shown me so many things
Ah! You too must see them!'
The third bell had rung, indicating that the movie was about to
begin. I was sitting with three or four companions in the second class.
One of the friends sitting next to me said, "Mahashayji has not yet
come?"

"He must be having a *paan*.[1] He'll be here soon. Look, the comedy
shorts have begun." Having dismissed my friend's concern, I looked
at the screen, but this behavior of mine was contrary to the norms
prevailing in my group. Whenever we went out for fun or to a play
or movie, we always stayed together. Mahashayji, whose full name is
Shriramcharanji, is a very popular member of my group. All of us are
very fond of him because of his love of laughter and his high spirits.
The fun of the movie would have been spoilt if he had not come. Maha-

This story, "*Paalat*," first appeared in *Matvala* on July 19, 1924. The Hindi word
paalat can idiomatically refer to a viper nursed in one's bosom, and here refers
to one who is kept and nurtured, but is poisonous.
    1. *Paan* is a mouth freshener, consisting of condiments and sometimes in-
toxicants wrapped in a betel leaf. Eaten after and between meals, it also has
centuries' old erotic connotations, traditionally being offered as a prelude to
lovemaking.

shayji's comments were funnier than Charlie Chaplin's antics. Finally, my friend spoke again, "We all had *paan* together, so he couldn't have stopped for *paan*. I hope he hasn't got into a quarrel with anyone? Shall I go out and see?"

Somewhat annoyed by this interruption to my enjoyment of the shorts, I replied, "He must be on his way. He's not a kid. If he needs to, he can fight with a couple of guys. Why are you so worried? See what you have come here to see. Great! Now the scene is over. The lights are on — go and look for him."

All of us, still seated, began to scan the cinema for Mahashayji. In a moment, we saw him — sitting in the first class! "Why?" I was surprised. "We all bought second-class tickets together. Why is Maha-shayji sitting apart from us, in the first class? What's going on? Why did he change his ticket?"

I called out to Mahashayji, "Hey buddy! Why are you on your own?"

Mahashayji: "Sitting there strains my eyes."

I: "But you'd save some money by sitting with us. And our seats are not very far away from yours."

Mahashayji: "I don't care about the money. 'The body is indeed the instrument of dharma.'² Have a *paan*. Oh *paanwala*! Over here!"

Amazing! Beyond amazing! Mahashayji was never known to be so generous. Not that he never treated us to *paan*. He did, but only after much wrangling. But today he was offering a treat on his own! I asked the friend sitting next to me, "What's going on? What's happened to Mahashayji?"

"I think I've guessed what's happened to him. But I'm not sure. We'll ask when he comes over."

"What's your guess? Let's hear."

"Look at the seat that is three seats away from him, to his right."

I looked over, and said, "It's a boy. What do you mean?"

"Wait till the intercession and then hear what I mean. He's a very good-looking boy. Do you know whose son he is?"

---

2. Idiomatic, quoted in Sanskrit. He means that preserving bodily organs, in this case, the eyes, is vital to well-being.

"How would I know? Am I a schoolteacher or a headmaster? What do I care whose son he is?"

The movie started. The *paanwala*, instructed by Mahashayji, came over to our seats and gave us *paan*.

2.

As soon as the intercession began, we all surrounded Mahashayji. All together, we asked, "Well, what's going on?"

Mahashayji, smiling, replied to all of us at once:

"'Why do you ask how I am?

Do you ever find me well?'"

This answer did not content us. We bombarded him with questions.

"Meaning?"

"What does that mean?"

"What do you mean?"

Mahashayji said, "After a very long time, brothers —

'I too am devoted to the lock falling on someone's cheek,

I too am the prey of time, of the passing days and nights.'

It's been a long time since I saw such a beautiful sight."

One of us asked, "What sight? Have you fallen in love with a film star? Tell us who it is."

Mahashayji: "Films — to hell with films. Look there! He — he is the one who has stolen my heart."

He drew our attention to the boy. He was eating something at the snack bar. I slapped Mahashayji on the back and said, "What kind of dirty fellow are you? You joke around with boys?"

But the rest of my friends wholeheartedly sympathized with Mahashayji. Aniruddh said, "Yes, Mahashayji, you have good taste. He is definitely a *number one* chocolate."

Kalyanchandra said, "Where does he live, you old rogue?[3] This bird should not be allowed to fly away."

3. An Urdu term is used, *Ustad*, a master, teacher, or connoisseur.

Mahashayji went on, "Just look at his eyes. Oh my, they are so wonderful. It is of such eyes that the poet says,

'It is from those half-open eyes,
That the bud has learnt to open slowly.'"

Shivmohan responded, "Mahashayji, your verse is not the right one.[4] Bihari's couplet is more suited to the occasion:

'I have never seen eyes so enchanting.
God! Those eyes are like the eyes of a doe.'"

Mahashayji: "Perfect, perfect. Who did you say the poet was? You must write that one down for me! But wait, he's coming this way. Look, look:

'What is the effect of that waist so slender, so fine?
My mind is too coarse to contain it, what can I do?'

Fellows, we should introduce ourselves to him."

Aniruddh: "We should, but how? We can't just go and ask him where he lives. What will he think of us?"

Mahashayji: "I'll tell you a way. You snatch Shivmohan's hanky and run with it, and Shivmohan will chase you and run into him. Then we'll get to know him while apologizing."

I did not like Mahashayji's plan, but the majority was on his side. So I was unwillingly compelled to take part in the campaign. As decided, Aniruddh took Shivmohan's hanky and ran towards the boy, and Shivmohan, running behind him, collided with the boy and knocked him to the ground. As soon as he fell, Mahashayji pounced on that boy-bird like a hawk. He helped him get up, and used his scarf to dust off the boy's clothes. He angrily said to Shivmohan, "You are very rude to treat a decent person like this!!"

Shiv folded his hands to the boy and said, "*I am very sorry. Please forgive me, brother! I knocked into you by mistake.*"

---

4. The word translated as "verse" is the Urdu *sher*. All the couplets so far quoted are in Urdu. Shivmohan now proceeds to quote Hindi poet Bihari (ca. 1595–1664), known for his erotic verse of the *riti* school. The couplet quoted is famous for two clever puns.

3.

The next day, Mahashayji's servant came to tell me that Maha-shayji had invited all of us to his house at five that evening. He had written a note to insist upon my going. I wanted to talk to him about the incident at the cinema the previous day. So I arrived at his door at four-thirty. I heard him singing this Urdu poem as he sat in his room:

"'Look at that glance like an arrow, look at the wounded heart,
Look at this looking, look at its result.
My heart wishes you to look at its condition.
It's left to you—look wherever you want.'"

Hiding at the door of the living room, I looked at Mahashayji's face. He seemed to be lost in the joy of song. Intoxication in his eyes, pathos in his voice, and blind love in his attitude! After singing two couplets of the *ghazal*, he paused for a moment as if thinking. After a deep sigh, he began singing again:

"'Why ask me for a detailed account?
Look at my flowing tears, look at the walls and the door.
You have been in love with yourself for years—
Look at the whole story condensed into this.
You are right in saying that my heart desires you
Wherever you look, you break many hearts.
Having given my heart to a beauty, I never loved anyone else—
Look at me in this state, and keep looking all life long.'"

I realized that Mahashayji's waves of love would not recede for a while, so I quietly entered the room.

After the usual greetings, I asked, "Why are you so sad today?"

Mahashayji: "Brother, I feel as if 'someone is crushing my heart today.'"[5]

"Whom else have you invited?"

Mahashayji: "Everyone from our group, and also our new friend from yesterday."

5. Inner quotation marks in original.

"Who?"

Mahashayji: "The one from the cinema."

"You've become so friendly with him! What's his name?"

Mahashayji: "A very beautiful name. Thinking of his name calms my heart. His name is Harisundar Varma.[6] He is the son of the local deputy collector, Mr. Rammanohar Varma."

"But you have never been acquainted with Mr. Rammanohar Varma's family. How did you become so fond of each other so soon? Just by colliding in the cinema?"

Mahashayji: "No, no, the cinema had nothing to do with it. We have hearts, we know how to love. Whomever we look at becomes our slave. There is such a thing as *will power*."

"Do you call this love? Unfortunate love must be wondering how it got involved with you. A man to love a man for his beauty! Brother, I think that just as 'a woman is not charmed by a woman's beauty,' so too it should be said that 'a man is not charmed by a man's beauty.'"[7]

Mahashayji: "But the world can't run only according to your thinking. Truth must be respected wherever it is. Beauty alone is truth. So whether the beauty is a woman's or a man's, 'I am a slave of love.'"[8]

"Your arguments may be correct. But this is a misuse of education."

Mahashayji: "Look through history. Your Raskhan, dying with love for a boy, finally became a devotee of Krishna.[9] Surdas would have given a hundred lives for Krishna.[10] Tulsi? Have you read the blazon

6. Harisundar: the beautiful God Vishnu. Mahashay's claim that thinking of this name calms his heart echoes the idea that dwelling on any of the names of God calms the heart.

7. The first phrase in quote marks is a quotation from *Ramcharitmanas* by the famous poet Tulsidas (ca. 1532–1623); the second is Ugra's adaptation.

8. The phrase in quotes is idiomatic in Urdu.

9. Raskhan (ca. 1533–1588) is the pen name of a medieval Muslim poet, who, according to legend, transferred his love from a beautiful boy to Shri Krishna.

10. Surdas (ca. 1479–1581) was a medieval devotional poet who, according to legend, was blind.

of Ram's beauty in *Vinaypatrika*?[11] What is that if not a portrait of an extremely beautiful boy?"

"Be quiet! You seem a regular atheist. To justify your love of boys, you drag in even Lord Ramchandra and Shri Krishna.[12] It's lucky you are sitting in your own room. If you presented such arguments in any public meeting, it would become impossible to protect the hair on your head."

Without answering me, Mahashayji once again began to sing:

"'My bee, the dark one, is a thief.

The beautiful one stole my heart with a sidelong glance.'"[13]

4.

Dusk fell. Lights were turned on in the room. All of our other friends arrived, but the gentleman who had stolen Mahashayji's heart did not turn up. What had happened? Could it be possible that he would not come? Kalyanchandra said to Mahashayji: "Well, it's no good waiting any longer. Let's start eating and drinking. Doesn't look like your Harisundarji will come."

"He won't come!" exclaimed Mahashayji sorrowfully. "Well, then, it's all a waste:

'If my beloved does not pour the wine, what good is the wine cup?

Empty the tavern though peopled with spirits!'

Without him . . ."

At that moment, a voice was heard at the door. "He's here!" I exclaimed. And it really was he. His get-up was worth looking at. An embroidered *kurta* of Bengali muslin, a velvety embroidered silk *dhoti* worn in a strange fashion, fine pump shoes, a wristwatch, a cap placed

---

11. A collection of devotional verses by Tulsidas in praise of Shri Ram.

12. The narrator uses the somewhat derogatory Urdu word *launda* for "boy." *Launda* has associations with *laundebaazi* (boy love). Mahashayji uses the Hindi word *larka* for "boy."

13. A famous verse in Brajbhasha by Surdas. The dark one is Shri Krishna.

aslant![14] As he entered he said to Mahashayji: "Forgive me — I'm very late."

Mahashayji: "Oh, please don't worry. You've come — that's all that matters. Do sit down, please."

Mahashayji seated Harisundar on his own chair; then he placed another chair right next to him and sat down there. We proceeded to eat and drink, laugh and sing; but through it all the state of that gathering was:

'Where he is, that is where everyone looks.

As for me, I look at the way the admirers look.'

Whoever Harisundar happened to glance at would appear extremely gratified! Everyone would envy that person's good fortune. At eight-thirty we all began preparing to return to our homes. Along with us, Harisundar also took leave of Mahashayji. But after bidding all of us goodbye, Mahashayji held "Hari" back, saying: "I'll walk you home. Stay a little longer."

5.

That day, Mahashayji did not join us. For two or three months, he had become hard to find. He was always occupied with his beloved Hari. Starting a discussion about Mahashayji and Harisundar, I asked Shivmohan, "How do these boys get caught in this swamp of sin?"

"Through the wiles of those who are better educated and older than themselves. Boys rarely become wicked on their own. Older people generally inspire them to be wicked."

"How?"

"By making them kept boys. By making selfish sacrifice appear like true sacrifice. They take boys to plays and movies, feed them snacks

14. His *dhoti* (cloth wrapped round the waist and drawn up between the legs, traditional Hindu male attire) is made of *pota*, a particular kind of silk embroidered with gold thread, usually used for Muslim women's *ghararas*. His *kurta* is *chikan*, a kind of embroidery usually done on muslin.

and ice cream! They present them with fine handkerchiefs and do all kinds of things for them. And then, our society too wants to prevent boys from doing many things that adults openly do. A father will wear perfume but tell his son not to wear it. He'll go to cinemas, theaters, and brothels but stop the boy from even eating *paan*. Such boys explode as soon as they find the slightest breach. They become bad charactered. Has Mahashayji told you the story of how Harisundar was caught?"

"No."

"According to Mahashayji, Harisundar gets very little pocket money from home. Just three or four rupees a month. Our Mahashayji began taking Hari to the movies, and spending fifties, if not hundreds, of rupees on him. And he also kept demonstrating his love. He would drink water left in Hari's glass and eat from his plate. He would whisper in his ear. Hari felt indebted to him on account of the money he spent. His moral downfall began. One day, Mahashayji asked him, 'Do you trust me?'

Hari: 'Why not? Who wouldn't trust you?'

Mahashayji: 'You do not consider me a cheat or a rogue, do you?'

Hari: 'O God! How can you say such things? Do you consider me so low? Even if you behave badly to me, I can never say anything bad about you.'

"What then? Still talking, Mahashayji kissed him and said:

'I kissed him and tricked him wonderfully . . .

I obtained pardon on the plea that this was a first offence.'

"Then he said, 'A kiss is a pure symbol of love. A mother kisses her child from pure love. A brother gives his younger brother or sister a pure kiss.'

"From that day, Mahashayji would regularly give Harisundar pure kisses."

I said, "Ugh! What a terrible murder of love! What a frightful downfall of the heart! What a great insult to humanity!"

"Although in this matter I consider myself weak like Mahashayji, still I don't hesitate to say that the present generation is being ruined. Boys who should be busy exercising are instead in solitary rooms learning to 'cry aloud' (who knows what it means to cry aloud?)[15] Those who should be learning to use the sword are casting "arrowlike glances." I think fifty percent of boys in the country and ninety percent in some regions are destroying their characters, virility, and strength in a terrible way. And society is silent. Reformers gaze on in wonder! I can say with certainty that boys should not be sent to modern schools and colleges even if it means their remaining uneducated. It is today's educational institutions that give rise to this bad education."

6.

After a long time, I encountered Mahashayji, who looked sad. I asked, "Why do you look so out of sorts?"

Mahashayji: "He's ill."

I: "Who? Hari?"

Mahashayji: "Yes, he is very seriously ill."

I: "Why are you not with him then, if he is sick?"

Mahashayji: "He failed his last exam. He was sick even during the exam. When he failed, someone complained of me to his father. Since then, I don't go to his house and he can't come to see me because he is ill."

I: "What's happened to him?"

Mahashayji: "T.B.! He's withered up, become skin and bone."

I decided to confront Mahashayji, and said, "All this must have happened because of you. You ruined that poor fellow! Yuck!"

Somewhat annoyed, Mahashayji said, "How did I harm him? I spent a huge amount of money on him. He himself is mischievous. You don't know these sons of rich men. They're very cunning."

15. The word used is *ghokhana*, a dialect variation of *ghoshana*, derived from Sanskrit, meaning to roar or cry, to preach, proclaim, or recite. The speaker professes uncertainty as to its meaning. It appears to be a sexually charged euphemism for crying out while having sex. There may be a pun on *gu khana* (literally, to eat excrement; figurative, to do something vile or shameful). Thanks to Saleem Kidwai for this latter suggestion.

I said, "That's enough. No need to justify yourself. You're a demon, an animal in human form. It's sinful even to look at your face. Please do not come to my house in future. I also have sons. Who would kill his sons by having them become 'chocolates' or 'kept' boys."

*   *   *   *

The next day, I heard the news of Harisundar's death. I struck my forehead and cried, "Unfortunate Hari! Murderous society!!"

WE ARE IN LOVE WITH LUCKNOW

1.

We were both teachers in a high school in Lucknow. It would be like fighting a corpse with a sword if I were to publish his name. I will call him Prasad Babu here. Although Prasad Babu and I had been classmates in college for a long while, I was senior to him as a teacher. Prasad Babu had failed twice in the B.A. That is how I passed the L.T.[1] and became a teacher two years before he did.

As soon as he was appointed to my school, I remembered his old habits and said to him, "Look, brother, this is a school. Teachers have a lot of responsibility. It will be disastrous if you continue to live here as you did when you were a student in school and college. And you'll also be ruined. Teachers' lives are beautiful only if they are naturally simple and pure. Teachers of small children are the life of the nation."

He smiled, and replied in the old tone that I knew well, "Harihar! You've lived all your life in Delhi but have wasted your time. You are the same simpleton you were in college. My people's goal in life is happiness. We will try to enjoy ourselves even in hell. If I planned to live like a sage, why would I have come to this poor school? There are

This story, "*Hum Fidaye Lakhnau*," was first published in *Matvala* on September 6, 1924.
1. Licentiate in Teaching

dozens of schools, but none of them has a collection of 'chocolates' like this one. And that is my life. I'm a true worshiper of beauty. I'll be found wherever beauty is. That is why I've come here. As long as I stay, I'll enjoy myself."

Even when I loathe a man's weakness, I still consider him human. This is my nature. And, after all, Prasad Babu was my friend too. I said, "All right, brother, I've done my duty. It's up to you. No friend, however dear, can care as much for your welfare as you yourself do. Who does not have vices? But vices can be hidden only if they are skillfully practiced. Do as you like, but guard your reputation and status."

Without replying, Prasad Babu looked at me, smiled, and began to sing,

"'Lucknow is in love with us,
We are in love with Lucknow.'"

2.

Within eight months, Prasad Babu became as talked about in our school as a ghost would be. The boys had their own view of him and their teachers a different view. One day, during the break, the teachers began to talk about him while he was not there. One said, "He's a terrible man. He doesn't care about the school, the headmaster, his reputation or his job. He's always after the boys. How long can this be allowed to go on?"

At this, the elderly Sanskrit teacher, Pandit Jagdambashastri, stuffing a pinch of snuff up his large nostrils, spoke up. "It's like this, it's all because this is the *kaliyug*.[2] As soon as boys acquire the badge of a B.A., it's like this, they are ready to kick at the sky. In love with boys! Govind! Govind!! It's like this, in what kind of hell can he find a place?"

2. The present era, the fourth and worst in the Hindu cycle of four eras. When one cycle ends, the universe is destroyed and another cycle begins with a new creation.

The history teacher, Mr. Ghandekar, added, "This fellow is a past master of the art. He traps the boys in his snare of sacrifice and love. But only the good-looking ones, mind you. The handsome ones are always monitors in his classes. The nice-looking ones get away with two tender slaps on the cheek and an *order* to *stand upon the bench*. In his regime, the unfortunate ugly ones can expect only death."

Another spoke up to second Mr. Ghandekar: "He even intercedes with the headmaster for the beautiful ones. I really hate him. I've taught here for twelve years, but I've never had a rascal like him as a colleague before. If he carries on like this, the school will soon become notorious. Harihar Babu! He says he's a friend of yours; why don't you speak to him? Tell him that for a teacher to lose his character is like playing with fire."

Just then, everyone's eyes were drawn with disgust towards Prasad Babu, who was passing the teachers' sitting room. He was not alone; with him were four or five beautiful, lively boys!

3.

The annual exams were almost over. All the teachers had received exam papers to be graded. This is the time when students begin to worship their teachers. Their salutations drip with devotion, and their conduct with solemn courtesy.

It was evening. It was Sunday and I was feeling restless, having stayed home all day. I thought I would go over to Prasad Babu's for a chat.

I walked straight into his house, but what was this? Why was the door of his study locked from within? The light was on. I quietly went up to the door and stood there. I could clearly hear two people's voices. I stood with my ear to the door.

Somebody inside whispered, "So, what will happen now?"

"What will happen? How does it matter if you fail this year?"

"Look, look, Master Saheb, I beg you! Please don't make a joke of this. If I fail, my family will make my life miserable."

"Well, if that bothers you, why didn't you come to me before? See-ing you bowing and scraping now makes me want to . . ."

Then someone said in an agitated, tender voice, "What is this? What are you doing? Your teeth will leave marks. Oh! My nose!!! Move away . . . ! Yes, yes. Oh! There are tooth marks on my cheek. Let me look in the mirror. You—what is this you are doing?"

It sounded as if someone had come down from the dais and was walking about the room. Then I heard the same voice, "You have bitten very hard, Master Saheb. If someone asks, what will I say?"

"Say you lay with your cheek on the edge of the bed, and that left a mark. Come here."

"First tell me, how will I pass Harihar Babu's course?"

Hearing my name, I realized that Prasad Babu was collecting inter-est on my friendship. He replied, "Come here first, no need to worry about Harihar Babu."

"Why? Will he do as you ask? Tell me the truth, Master Saheb."

"Come here first. If you stay far away, I won't tell you anything."

"I'm coming." The one with the tender voice took a couple of steps and perhaps sat down on the dais. "Here I am, now tell me."

"I can see that you pass Harihar Babu's course, but what will I get in return?"

There was no answer. Perhaps catching hold of the boy's hand, the teacher said, "Sit comfortably. Lie down if you want. I treat boys as my friends."

"I'm comfortable. Tell me. It's getting late. Father will be angry."

"Promise me that during the summer vacation you will come to my house once a day. Well?"

"I'll come—I'll try."

"No trying—say clearly, with your head on my chest, 'I will come.'"

I could not restrain myself any more. I called out, "Prasad Babu!" and pushed the door. The door was only stuck, not locked. As soon as I pushed, it opened. Prasad Babu and a boy from the seventh grade were on the dais together, mixed like milk and water. I acted like a curdling agent. As soon as he saw me, the boy jumped off the platform, and stood apart. My eyes were flashing. With a disgusted glance at Prasad Babu, I said to the boy, "Dularey!"

"Yes, sir."

"Come out for a minute. It's urgent. Prasad Babu, excuse me for a moment, I'll be back."

I had a walking stick in my hand. When we emerged from Prasad Babu's house, I caned Ramdularey dozens of times. He was too ashamed to utter a cry. Then I said, "Go home at once! Don't you dare come to Prasad Babu's so late at night. I will talk to your father tomorrow. Good for nothing fellow!"

4.

I didn't go into that base friend's house again. It was just as well. Who knows what I might have done in that fit of anger! I went straight home and began to look through the seventh-grade history papers. I graded Ramdularey's paper first of all. The first question was, "What do you know about Shaista Khan?" Ramdularey had written, "Shaista Khan was the oldest son and general of the famous Jahangir who built the Taj Mahal. He used deception to kill Shivaji in the Bijapur battleground. Once, Shaista Khan's daughter was very ill and was cured by a foreign doctor. As a reward, the doctor asked permission for the British to trade in India. At Shaista Khan's request, Jahangir opened the door to British trade in India."[3]

I marked this answer with a big Zero and turned the page to look at the next question when Prasad Babu appeared. As soon as he entered, he asked, "Why did you go away without meeting me?"

I decided against forgiving him any more, and replied, "You are not a man fit to be met with. Pardon me, but our friendship is over from today. I consider it a sin to maintain any contact with such rogues and demons."

Prasad Babu: "What are you saying? It's impolite to insult a decent person in your house."

3. Every sentence is absurdly inaccurate.

I: "Decent person? You? You vagabond! I've told you, our friendship is over. Tomorrow, when school reopens, a campaign will begin against you and I'll be the leader of that campaign. Wait and see!"

Prasad Babu: "You seem to be unwell today. That's why you are talking nonsense."

I: "Very well. Leave my house now, or I'll have to call a servant. Aren't you ashamed? You demon, a teacher destroying boys' character! In what hell will you find a place?"

Seeing me get extremely excited, Prasad grew afraid.[4] His face turned pale. In an affectionate tone, he said, "All right, brother, forgive me this time. But look, don't fail Ramdularey, just this once . . ."

I caught Prasad's hand, shoved him to the door and said, "Get going. You wicked fellow!"

5.

Prasad Babu was unable to keep his job, once all the teachers united against him. He was expelled from the school three days after this incident. It became difficult for him to continue living in Lucknow. Wherever he went, people pointed fingers at him. Everyone now knew that he was a follower of roses,[5] a demon in human form, an animal. Finally, that rogue was forced to run off to Calcutta to earn his bread.

* * *

A year ago, I read a news report in the *Statesman* from Calcutta:

"Prasad. . . . , from Lucknow, was a tutor at the home of a local businessman, Seth. . . . . One day, when alone, he did . . . . with the businessman's son! The rogue has been sentenced to seven years' rigorous imprisonment."

4. The adjective translated here as "extremely excited" is *ugra*, the author's pen name.

5. *Paatalpanthi. Paatal* in Brajbhasha is a rose or a trumpet flower. Here, it appears to be a code word.

When I read this report, I said, "Why wasn't he hanged? Such human animals should get the death sentence. Go, son! Grind grain and sing songs.[6] Now you'll realize the terrible consequences of sin! I trust you'll no longer sing, 'Lucknow is in love with us, we are in love with Lucknow.'"

6. Prisoners were often made to grind grain, and would sing as they did so.

Waist Curved Like a She-Cobra

1.

Like other theatrical companies, that company too gave its actors and audiences one day a week to rest. No plays were performed on Fridays; instead, the theater hall was used to show films. The actors who shouted their lungs out the whole week on stage rested to their hearts' content on Fridays. One would roam the streets till ten at night, another would try out the prostitutes of Dal ki Mandi, a third would sit with a new circle of friends and listen to their praise of his acting skills, and a fourth who had nothing better to do would sit alone and drink. Some would settle down in the theater hall. The Friday crowd in the cinema was rather large, because that is where the fashionable crowd, the sweethearts from the schools, would go to get better acquainted with the theater people. The men about town would get to meet theater prostitutes in the cinema on Friday, and would also find many theatrical chocolates! They preferred the chocolates, because it was easy to talk to them, and after getting familiar with them, even shake hands with them. Minds perverted by desire derive a type of restless satisfaction even from touch and from sweet talk, just as one who can knock back bottle after bottle enjoys even a cup or two of wine.

This story, "*Qamariya Nagin Si Bal Khaye*," was published in *Matvala* on December 6, 1924.

"The movie's not over yet. Hang on—why don't you listen? Why did you insist on bringing me here if you wanted to leave halfway through?"

Pulling me towards him, Harnarayan said, "Oh buddy, why are you harassing me? All my fun will be spoilt; the *program* will be ruined. Come on!"

I replied with some asperity, "What fun and what ruin? We've spent money on the movie; let's enjoy it fully. Let me see *Pearl White*'s smiling face once more."

"Into the furnace with your *Pearl White*. You've seen her thousands of times but you're still not satisfied. I won't let you sit here any longer. Come on out, I'll show you something that will send your spirits into a flutter and make you lose your senses: 'Come see the drama of God's nature.'[1] Come on."

I was forced to leave the cinema hall. Harnarayan Babu came out, stood at a tobacco stall, and said to me, "Tell him to prepare a very good *paan* with care while I look around for my prey . . ."

Suddenly looking towards the cinema hall, Harnarayan Babu lit up. "Look there, there he comes. Forget about the *paan*, we'll get it later. Come with me."

Harnarayan dragged me along towards the crowd that was emerging from the cinema hall and walking southwards. After walking fast for about three minutes, he slowed his gait and said, "Look, there he is. This is a good opportunity. Let's stop him. Don't worry, I'll take care of everything. You just stand quietly."

Moving forward, Harnarayan Babu called out, "Oh sir! A moment, please."

As I approached, I saw that Harnarayan Babu's "sir" was a young actor from the theater. His tongue dripping with the sweetness of his heart, Babu Saheb said, "Is your good name Ramu?"[2]

"Yes—why? Who are you?"

---

1. Urdu quotation.
2. It is customary in Hindi, when asking someone's name, to attach the adjective *shubh* (auspicious or good) to the noun "name."

"I just asked, because your talent is so great that everyone's eyes are fixed on you. Today there is no performance—why are you in such a hurry? Do have a *paan* with us."

"*Paan?* Sure, I don't mind. But, as you know, we are not independent. The people in charge of the theater don't allow us to associate with outsiders."

"Who's in charge here? I know many actors and managers of this company. No one will be annoyed with you. Do come this way."

We went back to the tobacco stall. That boy, Ramu, really was very good looking. His large eyes, high cheekbones, and shoulder-length wavy hair were very attractive. The *paan* shop owner looked at Ramu and smiled; the passers-by looked at him and at us as if we had just caught a golden bird. We began to talk.

Harnarayan (to Ramu): "Do you have relatives in this company?"

Ramu: "Yes, my father is also in this company. He plays the part of Taufiq in *Khubsurat Bala*."[3]

Harnarayan: "Oh, he's a very talented actor. You are Gujaratis, aren't you?"

Ramu: "Yes, we are Gujarati Brahmans from Ahmedabad district."

Harnarayan (giving Ramu a *paan*): "Here you are, have a *paan*. But your father must be allowed to go out freely? The company managers wouldn't restrict older actors, would they?"

Ramu (eating *paan*): "Father is free to go out, and he can take me with him if he likes. Well, pardon me but I must be going now, it's getting late."

Harnarayan: "Yes, of course. Sorry if we caused you any trouble. You're like a younger brother to me. Tomorrow I'll introduce myself to your father, and then I will invite you both to my humble abode. You'll come, won't you?"

Ramu: "If Father agrees, I have no objection."

"Oh, what's this?" Harnarayan Babu gently touched Ramu's cheeks two or three times with his handkerchief. "There is some lime on your chin."

3. Title of a Parsi play. Literally, *The Beautiful Girl*.

2.

I understood what he was after. Although I had long known that Harnarayan Babu was a rogue, I had not expected him, at the age of thirty, to pursue "chocolates." I was upset to see how attracted he was to Ramu. On the way home, I said to him, "This must be what they mean by being ever-youthful, right?"

"What do you mean?" he asked in a somewhat displeased manner.

"This habit of boy-love.[4] Do you know what society thinks of these theater people?"

"I don't care about society. Society is foolish and blind. Why should I destroy my happiness because of society?"

"You call this happiness? Yuck! Society and the law both call it a sin and it is really a terrible sin, yet you call it happiness? Ram, Ram!"

"People like you, who belong to the eighteenth century, think that way," replied Harnarayan Babu. "My principle is the worship of beauty. I am attracted to beauty wherever I see it. I am a slave of love."

"So you really mean to ensnare Ramu?"

"Most certainly. Didn't you see what a beautiful, murderously enchanting chocolate he is? Can anyone resist such a thing?"

"That will be a sin."

"You may think it a sin, but I think it something else. You and I define sin differently. Why quarrel about this? Just watch the fun. Even if I have to spend thousands, I'll definitely invite Ramu to my house at least once:

'All night long, it is impossible to sleep because of this separation
This pain in the heart has become a threat to my life.'"[5]

4. Unusually, Ugra here uses the Sanskrit term, *batuk prem*, rather than an Urdu term or the term "chocolate lover."
5. Urdu couplet.

All of Harnarayan's friends were gathered together. This gathering was in honor of Ramu's visit to his house. Everyone had partaken of opium, Ramu's father Gopal had sung a song, and we had also heard a devotional song in Ramu's tender voice. When Ramu's song ended, his father said, "We'll take leave of you now; it's nearly eight. We have to snatch a few moments to rehearse, too."

Before Harnarayan could reply, a Muslim friend of his spoke up, "Well said! Do you folks snatch moments or our lives?"

Harnarayan whispered something in my ear and then said to Ramu's father, "Please eat something before you go. It's important to eat and drink after taking opium."

"That's true," Gopal said politely. "But one feels sleepy after eating and can't act with vigor. So please excuse us."

Harnarayan: "Well, no need to eat if you'd rather not. I won't eat now either. But do let him (Ramu) eat something."

"Yes, yes," Gopal turned to Ramu. "If you feel like drinking water eat something, but don't eat so much that you get indigestion. We have to serve our employer too."

Ramu looked embarrassed, and everyone started laughing. Asking Ramu to get up, Harnarayan said to me, "Snacks are laid out in the next room. Please accompany him there."

Everyone else remained seated in the outer room. The dining room was next door, but no one could see Ramu there. He ate slowly, and I walked around the room, observing his innocent face. I pitied the boy's simplicity and was angry at Harnarayan's wicked conspiracy. While Ramu was eating, Harnarayan appeared and said, "Shall I demonstrate the truth of what I whispered to you?"

I: "Oh, let it alone. You're a strange man."

Harnarayan: "What's strange about it — Ramu will agree with what I said."

Still eating, Ramu said, with a smile, "What did you say?"

Harnarayan: "First finish eating, then I'll tell you."

When he finished eating, Harnarayan said, "You must eat a *paan* from my hand. This is what I wanted to persuade you to do."

Without replying, Ramu stood, with his head bent, wiping his mouth with his handkerchief. Harnarayan went up to him, *paan* in hand, and said, "Here you are, look up."

The innocent Ramu raised his head, and Harnarayan stuffed four *paans* into his mouth, but alas! the redness of the *paan* spread over his face! His cheeks and ears turned red from shyness. Before feeding him the *paan*, Harnarayan had kissed Ramu's lips!!!

* * * *

When the two actors had left, all of Harnarayan's friends raised a ruckus about the way he had managed the food. Mohammad Siddique said, "Wonderful, sir! You slipped into the dining room and cut the sweet potato all alone? And we were left hungry like a stepmother's son! Great, my friend, great!"

Siddique's words seemed to set my body on fire. I said, "Look, sir, I don't like this type of behavior."

"Why would you like it?" said another friend of Harnarayan's, a schoolteacher. "The pleasures of the dining room cannot be found in our conversation! No need to put on an act with us. After eating seventy mice, the cat goes on pilgrimage."[6]

I said, "Mind your tongue. I can't put up with such talk."

Master: "If you can't, close your ears. None is taken in by you. Go pretend to be pure before those who don't know you. This farce won't work with us."

I could not take any more of this. I clenched my fist and sprang towards that wicked teacher, but Harnarayan Babu intercepted me, saying, "Why are you playing the policeman? If you don't like something, stay away from it. Come on, have a bite to eat before we go to the theater. I've decided to give a '*gold medal*' to Ramu and his father."

---

6. Idiomatic, a hypocritical sinner who pretends to be pious.

4.

Harnarayan's whole gang of witches went with him to the theater. All of them sat in the "*orchestra*," and Harnarayan bought all the tickets. The episode of the dining room and the debate with that wicked teacher were preying on my mind. A fearsome flame of revenge blazed in my heart. I turned my eyes away from those wicked fellows. I sat quietly, sometimes looking towards the stage and sometimes towards the gallery. Suddenly, someone called from behind, "Mohan Ji!"

I looked back at the person who had called out, and so did the others. It was my friend, the police inspector of my neighborhood. I went over to where he was seated. After an exchange of pleasantries, he asked, "Who are the others with you? You've come with a big crowd!"

I: "They're all rascals, sir. They've all come here chasing after a boy."[7]

He (surprised): "Your friends are chasing a boy? Is everything all right?"

I: "If you can somehow straighten them out, everything will be all right."

He: "How can I do that? Is there any evidence?"

I spoke quietly in his ear. "The day after tomorrow, there will be a big secret party at Harnarayan Babu's house. If you come with a police posse to that party, you'll catch them. But one thing—please don't arrest anyone. You may punish them as you like."

"Fine, I'll do that," he replied. "Let me know when the time is right. I won't be far away."

Just then, the play began.

* * * *

An Indian play, and the Parsi stage. Ninety-nine percent of Indian writers' plays become like red chilis added to peppers when they are played on the Parsi stage. The play we were watching was of that type too. Its humor was disgusting and bizarre, like a stream of obscenity.

7. The word used here for boy is *launda*.

Ramu played the role of Mr. Quarrelsome's wife in the "*comic*" part of the play. Whenever he came onstage, all the spectators went wild.

In her husband's absence, Mr. Quarrelsome's wife (Ramu) began to meet another man. Oh God! Oh God!! The scenes between them were nothing but kissing and embracing. Watching those scenes, the devilish audience kept yelling, "Oh lord! You are killing me!" When Ramu began to sway his waist and dance to the tune of "The waist curves like a she-cobra," I could no longer bear the spectators' obscene cries. I got up and left for home.

People will do and put up with all kinds of things for money.

5.

There was a big hall in Harnarayan Babu's house. Arrangements for the party had been made there. Pleased with the money he had received, Ramu's father Gopal had arranged for Ramu to join the assembly in women's attire, and to dance and sing the song, "Waist curved like a she-cobra." A curtain was hung in the middle of the hall. The group of devils sat in front of the curtain, and behind the curtain Gopal began to make up Ramu as a woman.[8] Before the party started, Harnarayan's group had drunk to their heart's content. All the friends were tipsy.[9]

The party began. Gopal started playing the harmonium, and Ramu began to dance and sing. The bunch of friends started their usual caterwauling. Trembling with intoxication, Harnarayan said to me, "Look, if you don't like what we are up to, you can leave. Today I'm determined to fulfill all my desires. Don't you see:

'With what style he has come to my house,

8. The term translated as "devil" is the Urdu *shaitan*, Satan. The term earlier translated as "demon" was the Sanskrit *rakshasa*. Rakshasa does not have the same connotations of eternal damnation that Satan does.

9. The word used for "friends" is *yaar*, which can also mean "lover," depending on the context. The primary meaning here is "friend," but the secondary meaning is also suggested.

Somewhat reserved, modest, and somewhat shy.'"

I said, "Be quiet, Harnarayan Babu. Don't go mad, don't get rid of your humanity."[10]

"Ha ha ha ha!" Harnarayan laughed. "Humanity? Where is humanity? Call her before me. I will beat that bastard humanity hundreds of times with my shoes! Ha ha ha ha!

'Tell the breeze to come quickly and blow out the lamp.

Several veiled ones have arrived here.'"[11]

The wicked Mohammad Siddique spoke up to excite Harnarayan further: "Why wait any longer, sir? The wine, the goblet, the wine pourer, and the cup, all are here — what do you say?"[12]

"Ha, ha, ha," replied the intoxicated Harnarayan.

'The impatient heart would wreak havoc, but so far

I restrain it, hold it back, distract its attention.'"

Having said this, Harnarayan stood up and looked at Ramu with thirsty eyes! Demonic emotions played in his eyes; he was completely mad. In a moment, everyone saw him pick up Ramu and walk towards the curtain, crying out,

'You will not find it again, take it when you can,

The impatient heart has been waiting so long.'"

*   *   *   *

Behind the curtain, Ramu cried aloud, "Oh! Oh!" and outside sat his base father, running his hand over the harmonium. Harnarayan's other friends also went behind the curtain. I stood alone outside, perturbed, hoping for the police to attack!

Just then, my friend the police inspector entered the hall with fifteen to twenty policemen! My heart swelled with gladness on seeing

10. The word used is the Urdu *aadmiyat*; its primary meaning is "humanity," but its secondary meaning, "manhood," is suggested. The word is gendered feminine, which leads to its personification as a woman in Harnarayan's next speech.

11. In this Urdu couplet, the term "veiled one" would normally refer to women, but Harnarayan uses it to refer to the boy as object of desire.

12. All tropes from Urdu love poetry.

them. I said, "Inspector Saheb, beat those bastards a hundred times each with shoes! All of them are demons, devils in human form!"

* * * *

Shoe-beatings by the police compelled Gopal to send Ramu to study in Gujarat. Harnarayan's bunch of devils came to their senses, and the schoolmaster, too, had his head well knocked. After that day, Harnarayan never again dared get involved with the discussion of chocolate![13]

Shoes turned the fire of love to ashes.

13. The term used here is *chocolate charcha*, which is the title of the following story. See the footnote concerning that title.

Discussing Chocolate

Having supervised the porter who put my bedding and trunk in the train, I began strolling on the platform. So what if I was traveling third class? I was still a *gentleman*.[1] *Gentlemen* board the train only when it starts moving. At least that's the way *gentlemen* of my age in my country behave!

When the guard and the engine both whistled to assure us that the train was about to leave, someone called out to me from the compartment, "Get in, sir. The train is about to leave."

I: "I'll get in—there's no hurry."

He: "What's the use of wandering about like that? It's a crime to board a moving train."

I: "It may be a crime, but all the guards in the world are seen boarding trains only once they get moving. Isn't that a crime?"

He: "Come on, brother, why talk of guards? They're railway officials."

This story, "*Chocolate Charcha*," was first published in *Matvala* on December 13, 1924. The title in English retains the pun in the original. The primary meaning of *charcha* is to talk about or discuss, with an implied meaning of practicing an activity. A secondary meaning is to smear or spread something on the body, just as a secondary meaning of "discuss" is to consume something. I translate the word *charcha* in the story in various ways, depending on the context.

1. The word is in English in the original, which has a satirical effect.

Just then, the train whistled for the last time and started moving. I leapt on to the train, entered the compartment, and occupied my seat.

Having glanced round at my fellow passengers, I began reading my newspaper. Remember, *gentlemen* do not read *Leader, Forward,* or *Servant.*[2] They enjoy only the *Statesman* or the *Pioneer.* I was reading the *Statesman.* It is a characteristic of train passengers to do whatever others are doing. If one sings, all the rest hum along. If some people go to sleep, everyone prepares to sleep. Seeing me reading a newspaper, the rest decided to do so too. First of all, one man, who appeared to be from the United Provinces, took *Matvala* out of his pocket and began to read it. Before he had read a couple of pages, another man, who appeared to be highly orthodox, said to him, "Why do you read *Matvala?*"

"What do you mean? Do you consider *Matvala* an impure paper?"

"No doubt about it. It's probably the most impure paper not just in the Hindi world but even in the whole world. Have you ever noticed the discussion of chocolate in it?"

"Ever noticed it? Of course! I regularly notice it. So you consider *Matvala* the worst of all the world's papers just because it discusses chocolate? Ha ha ha ha! Looks as if you've only heard about the world but never seen any of its papers. You'd pass out if you saw some of the papers in Western countries. Why are you so unhappy about the discussion of chocolate in *Matvala?*"

"You ask why I'm unhappy? Can it ever be a good thing to preach such disgusting matters as chocolate in society?"

"*Matvala* is preaching?" The admirer of *Matvala* grew somewhat excited. "Our society itself is degraded. It knows well that many wicked beings are burdening its chest every day with the rocks of chocolate-love. Every child in this society knows what the practice of chocolate is. In every part of society there are wicked people who are predatory tigers by nature but who appear to be mild cows. What is

2. Names of nationalist newspapers.

poor *Matvala* doing but exposing such people? It should be thanked for doing so."

"It should be thanked?" responded the guardian of orthodoxy. "If it were up to me, I would hang all the writers and publishers who discuss chocolate. What's the use of shedding light on the wrong acts that society does secretly? Everyone is naked under the *dhoti*."[3]

"Society does not hide this weakness. Chocolate is openly practiced in schools, colleges, theater companies, and Ramlila groups.[4] So many good poets, writers, and great leaders are said to be prey to this illness."

"That is a lie, a deception. Society can never be so disgusting."

* * * * * * *

A handsome young man sitting near the window replied to the orthodox pundit, "Sir, you appear to be an inhabitant of an ancient Golden Age society. What you are calling a lie is absolutely true. For example, listen to my story."

Everyone in the compartment looked at the youth. He was about twenty-one or twenty-two years old, extremely attractive, with a shapely face, fair complexion, large eyes, and a high forehead. He went on: "I am a third year student in college. Thanks to God's wrath, there are very few nice-looking young boys in college. So if any student is even slightly good looking, most of the love-intoxicated fellows start chasing him. That's what happened to me.

"Wherever the older and in-the-know mischievous students saw me—in class, in the common room, in the field—they would show their colors by exclaiming, 'O Prince!' 'He's killing me!' '*Money order,*' '*Pocketbook,*' and so on.[5] I was fed up of constantly running away from my classmates, yet they kept bothering me. There are many dorms in

3. Idiomatic, meaning that we all have something to hide.
4. Itinerant religious theatre troupes in north India. See my discussion in the introduction of Ugra's account of his childhood experiences as an actor in one such troupe.
5. The author in his preface identifies the last two as slang terms for a man's younger lover.

that college. The boarding superintendent lived in my dorm. I complained to him several times, but he always claimed helplessness. He said these boys are adults who know very well what they are doing, so what's the use of reasoning with them? One day, in the superintendent's presence, a Punjabi student said to me, 'Sir, can you solve a math problem for me?'

'What is it?' I asked.

'Twenty-one plus two,' he replied.

I bit my lip in anger and kept quiet. The meaning of his twenty-one plus two was nothing but *'Give me a kiss.'*"

* * * * * * * *

"One day I was sitting in my room reading a book when a friend of mine came in and said, 'Dinkar! Run away! A big group of boys from the third dorm is coming here to harass you. Look there!'

"I was astonished at the sight I saw.

"About sixty or seventy boys carrying a corpse on a bier were yelling something as they approached my room. Seized with fear, I ran up to the superintendent's room. They all stopped at the door of my room and began to shout, 'Dinkar! Oh beautiful Dinkar! Waiting for you, your lover pined away and died.[6] If you come and touch him, he'll revive.'

"When they could not find me, they went off in search of some other beautiful boy. They found an unfortunate one somewhere, and dragged him to the bier. That boy was forced to touch the pretend corpse of the dead lover.

"The lover was just rising from the bier, beating his breast, when the college principal, hearing of the boys' mischief, arrived on the scene! When he witnessed that spectacle of the nation's students' degradation, he exclaimed, trembling with rage, 'You wretches! Aren't you

---

6. The word used for "waiting" is Firaq, the pen name of Raghupati Sahay "Firaq" Gorakhpuri (1896–1982), a major Urdu poet from Uttar Pradesh, whose homosexuality was well known.

ashamed to play such a degraded joke? All of you are a stain on this college.'

"The day after this episode, I removed my name from the college rolls. The day I left, I felt like crying over my beauty. In this degraded nation, it's a sin not only to be truthful, patriotic, and outspoken but even to be good looking."

* * * * * * * *

The orthodox pundit was stunned by the youth's narrative, and I said, "If you all do not think it improper, I would like to write a report of this incident and send it to the editor of *Matvala*."

The youth happily gave his consent.

O Beautiful Young Man!

1.

It was the dark half of the month. The light-filled empire of daytime's maiden had declined, and dark night reigned over the world. The peaceful, somber darkness of nature's heart was just beginning to blossom, the lamp posts in the Company Garden had not yet donned their crowns of shining light, when a group of ten to twenty students sitting on the lawn in one corner of the Garden heard a commotion.

"Perhaps it's a fight."

"Yes, it does sound like that — there, towards the south — near the fountain — can you hear it? *Yes, come on. Let us go there and see what is the matter.*"[1]

"Forget about it! Sit, I'll sing a *ghazal.* Someone must be getting his head broken — what has it to do with you?" So saying, one mischievous boy began to sing.

"Aa . .aa. .aa. aa. .aa. . . . !
You have given me pain, you heal me too —
Save me from the mercy of any other savior!"

This story, "*Hey Sukumar,*" first appeared in the book *Chocolate* in 1927, as the opening story. *Sukumar* means a handsome, beautiful, tender or delicate male youth.

1. I italicize words in English in the original.

But the boy could not sing the next verse. An acquaintance of theirs came running up, panting, and put an end to the fun.

"Mohan! O Mohan! Shyamu, O Shyamu! Come quickly. There's a huge drama going on. A big hullabaloo!"

"What is it? What's going on there?"

"Come on—you have to run! Come and see for yourself—it's a drama worth seeing."

One boy replied, "Yeah, let's go and see what's going on."

The singer retorted, "No, thanks. Why don't you listen to my song? Where are you running off to?"

A third said, "No, no, no. We must go."

All the boys stood up together and rushed towards the fountain with a whirr like a bunch of locusts.

2.

When they came close to the commotion and the crowd, the boys saw some people standing in a circle and raising a ruckus. Everyone was yelling, and they could not see what was going on in the middle of the circle. Finally, the boys, using their heads the way calves do, made their way through the crowd.

At the center of the circle they saw a weak, thin man with a short, thick, black beard, who was somewhat crazy in appearance,[2] wearing nothing but a dhoti and a shabby kurta, firmly holding the wrist of a Westernized dandy, whose face was pale with fear.[3] He looked stunned. Close to the eccentric fellow and the dandy stood a handsome young boy with neatly styled hair, who also looked ashamed and embarrassed.

2. This man is throughout referred to as *sanaki*, meaning crazy or eccentric. I use both words.

3. The other man is described as *chhaila* (modish, fine-looking, handsome, a dandy) and *shaukin*, which can mean amorous, a connoisseur, modish, or a fancier of particular pastimes, especially Western ways.

Someone in the crowd said to the eccentric fellow: "OK, now let him go, brother, pardon him, forget it."

"No, no, no," cried the crazy man, glaring around with red eyes. "I will beat this rogue to my heart's content. Ask him, all of you, why he was sitting on that bench under the tree with this boy? What is this boy to him? Let him prove some relationship—is he his brother, nephew, disciple, uncle? And if he is not related to him, then why was this rascal sitting in the dark, with his arm around the boy's neck? What was he doing?"

Suddenly, the eccentric fellow began showering slaps on the dandy. That fine fellow lost class; his cap sprang off his head and fell on the head of a street sweeper in the crowd. This time, though, he exerted all his strength and managed to free his wrist from the crazy man's grasp. Without an instant's delay, he rushed through the crowd like a dog with his tail between his legs and whizzed away into the darkness.

The boys began to shout, "Coward! He ran off! He's a chocolate-lover! Catch him, beat him, don't let him get away!"

3.

After the Westernized man ran away, the crazy one kept talking, "All you good men, listen to me! Whenever you see a loafer sitting with an unrelated boy in such solitary places, start to beat him up right away. If only a dozen of you start to beat those boy corrupters with shoes, the whole city will become pure. You deliberately try to cover up such things, but this is a futile approach. Sin does not disappear by being covered up; it grows stronger. These days our society has become very cruel and vicious towards boys, especially beautiful boys."

"But, brother, tell me one thing!" someone in the crowd asked. "Why are you so opposed to such people? Everyone will reap what he sows. Who are you to take the law into your own hands?"

"No," growled the crazy fellow. "When the law cannot help us, cannot control criminals and demons in society, it is our duty to take the law into our hands. I have suffered myself—these sinners set my house on fire. They wrenched out my heart. Shall I tell you my story? All right, listen.

"I too had a son. He was my only son. He was the joy of my life and the sweetness of my solitude. He was beautiful as the dawn and attractive like money. He studied at a school right here. A base demon of this city cast his evil eyes on him. Without my knowledge, he trapped my son with his sweet words, false love, and net of money. For years, he would take my child out here and there, and feed him ice cream and snacks. After this, the boy's health began to be ruined. Gradually tuberculosis got him in its clutches.

"At first I could not believe what the doctors told me after examining him. But it hardly mattered what I chose to believe or not believe. The doctors were right. My child had developed T.B. due to bad acts. He gradually decayed, withered, and died of that disease! Oh! The memory sets my heart on fire! My eyes begin to spit forth sparks."

The eyes of that crazy man actually filled with tears at the memory of the boy. He stopped for a moment, choked up.

Then he went on, "Finally I managed to find that sinful man. You may not have heard about this, but I disgraced him too in public. My opinion is that such men should be dishonored in the middle of the marketplace. It is not wrong or sinful to do this. Oh, my child!! My son!!!"

4.

Suddenly, the eccentric's eye fell on the eager group of boys. He smiled, and then grew solemn.

"Children!" he said. "Come here. Move, all of you, give way to these innocent tender beautiful playthings! Listen, I will tell you something.

"O beautiful young men! You do not yet know what this world is like. You are filled with enthusiasm and curiosity. You do not know the difference between good and bad. That is why I say to you, Do not consider my words a joke. This is not the age to learn bad things. You should not play the drama of love now; do not get seduced and hide your face on anyone's chest. Refrain from understanding the mysteries of embraces and kisses. Don't sell your beautiful bodies, your blossoming cheeks, your red lips!"

One adult student laughed at the eccentric's words. "This guy knows it all," he whispered in his companion's ear. "He's a master of the art. Seems to know everything about us."

"O beautiful boys!" the eccentric went on. "True love is not madly eager to embrace, kiss, or play in private, or to roam around clasping one's friend, regardless of good or evil. Such love is always — remember, always — impure.

"A friend of yours? It's a lie. At your age, one doesn't know the meaning of friendship. Your friendship is a wall of sand. And those who come to kiss or love you, pretending to be your friends or brothers, are never your friends. They are friends of their eyes and their mischievous hearts, friends of their idolatrous temperaments. They are jealous of your heavenly beauty and priceless purity. They flatter you to demolish your divinity. Save yourselves from such friends, whether they be your neighbors or relatives, teachers or elders!

"Don't bend your bodies before any blind friend, don't feel shy or pressured to do so. Once you bend, you will have to continue bending, and this fall will continue till you yourself become a demon like that sinful friend of yours. Don't become enslaved to your senses so early; don't turn yourself from a god into a demon. Otherwise, once this beauty is destroyed, this dazzling face is blackened, the redness of these fair lips dries up, the shyness of these eyes dies, you will face nothing but hatred and disgust in the world.

"These people do not love you and do not care about your welfare. They love your tenderness that is as hard to find as heaven, your beauty that is rare as the Gods', and your attractive vitality that is rare in the world. As soon as nature or men steal these from you, you will become three a penny. Then nothing but the black stains of your folly will be visible on the sheet of your life, and seeing them, everyone will hold his nose. Even those responsible for pushing you into bad ways will call you bad and think of you as bad.

"Exercise, eat, laugh, play, and study! This will make your future bright. Don't look for the meanings of 'friend' and 'darling' and 'lover' and 'master' and 'god' in the dictionary of the world so soon. You don't need these now. I'm telling you the truth. Don't think this a joke. Don't forget my words when you leave here.

"O beautiful youths! O beautiful ones!" As he went away from the crowd, the crazy man kept repeating. "O attractive ones! O pure ones! Again I say, Don't let any man kiss your lips, don't let any intoxicated one stroke your cheeks, don't let any demon press your tender chest to his iron heart![4] You are not sex objects. You are men, you are gods, you are God—always stay far from these sinners! O beautiful, O beloved, O tender ones, O light of families and lamp of homes! Be careful!"

4. This was the kind of explicit description that the opponents of *Chocolate* objected to as titillating.

Dissolute Love

1.

"I've found it! I've found it!!"

"What have you found, brother? Oho! You can hardly contain your joy! Have you found a buried treasure?"

"Buried treasure is nothing compared to the treasure I've found. I have found that wealth which billionaires throughout the world thirst for. Oho! Oho!! Don't speak, don't ask! Let me sink and swim in my happiness; don't ask for a part of it; don't try to share my joy. You're an old friend of mine, but I cannot give you, I don't want to give you even a particle of my heavenly riches."

"Don't give me a share, friend![1] But do at least tell me what this wealth is you have found? You have so much inherited wealth already, so what does this mean? What is this treasure you have acquired, which is making you dance with joy? Do tell me. I'm not going to snatch any of it. Oh! Doubt on your face again. What a strange thing! A friend like you to become so selfish as to fear even mentioning the name of your

This story, "Vyabhichari Pyar," first appeared in the book *Chocolate* in 1927.

1. The word used is *yaar*. Commonly used in modern colloquial Hindi as the equivalent of "buddy," the word has an illustrious poetic heritage, both hetero and homoerotic, with the meaning "male lover," (derived in part from Sanskrit *jara*, woman's adulterous lover), of which Ugra would have been aware.

new treasure! You silly fellow, I swear—I swear by you and by my own head—that I won't ask for a share. Now you can trust me and tell me its name. Or do you want me to swear some more oaths? Speak!"

"Unh hun, unh hun, unh hun!" said Kalyanchandra.[2] "I won't introduce you—or anyone else for that matter—to this wealth. Pardon me. This wealth is such that to tell anyone about having acquired it makes one feel that one has given the listener a share in it. I was wrong to mention it in front of you, but what could I do? I was compelled to do so, because I'm so used to telling you about all the ups and downs in my life. It was just out of habit that I spoke of this wealth. Forget what I said. I haven't found anything at all."

"Fine," said Devsingh. "Don't tell me. Good day, I'm off. If I don't stay here I won't keep asking you about it."

"No, no, don't go. And listen, listen! Come here. Sit down. Yes, that's good. I'll tell you. I can't stop myself from telling you! I've finally found that wealth without which I have been restless and unhappy. The poetry of my heart was dying and its blossom withering."

"Sir artist, tell me its name! Great poet! Sage of literature! End this useless preface! Have you exchanged glances with someone?"[3]

Kalyanchandra's eyes suddenly grew glazed. "You have guessed right—very clever of you. I have found my beloved.[4] I have found my ideal. I have attained my ideal of beauty, love and art. Now my heart is not a desert but a pleasure garden. I am not a beggar but a king—a king!"

"Who is this fortunate goddess, in finding whom you have attained the world's empire?[5] Where does she live?"

2. The sound indicates a negative response.

3. *Kisi se aankhen lar gayi hain*, literally, have your eyes met someone else's? This is a common idiom for mutual attraction.

4. Kalyan uses *pyara*, the masculine word for beloved. In Urdu poetry, this word is conventionally used for any beloved, male or female (see my discussion of this convention in the introduction). Heterosexism leads Devsingh to assume that the *pyara* is a woman.

5. *Devi*, literally goddess, is common polite usage to refer to a woman. Kalyanchandra gives the usage a poetic twist when he calls his beloved a god, even though men are not normally referred to as gods.

"You will laugh at what I say, you may even be disgusted, but I have to tell you. My ideal is not a goddess but a god—not a woman but a man, a boy."

"A boy!! What are you saying, Kalyan? Your ideal of love and beauty and art is a boy?"

"Yes, yes, he's a boy. I'm not hiding it from you. He's the shining lamp[6] in the hut of a poor man who lives on my estate. The father is my dependent. He couldn't afford to educate the boy so he gave him to me a while ago. I found the support of my life all of a sudden, as if God showered nectar down on the desert of my heart, breaking all barriers. He has just gone to the market. Come tomorrow and I'll show him to you. He's so innocent, so pure, so tender and beautiful, so intoxicating! Oh lord! As soon as his image comes before my eyes, I wax poetic."

"Do you love him?"

"How can you ask me that? Krishna could not have loved Arjuna as much or Chapla Ghanshyam as much as I have started loving him these last few days. Come in for a minute. I'll read you the poems I've recently written. I bet you'll swoon when you hear the song of my heart. Oh! After what anguish, after what a long wait have I met my beloved!"

2.

One day, some of Devsingh's friends surrounded him in the marketplace and asked him what had become of his friend Kalyanchandra. One asked, "Hey, sir, what are these rumors screaming about your friend? Yuck! What kind of friend are you? Why don't you try to reform him?"

Growing grave, Devsingh replied, "It is because I do not try to reform him that we are still friends. These days, a friend who becomes a reformer is immediately shown the door. If A is B's friend it means that A flatters B to the hilt. Friendship can't exist today without flattery."

6. The lamp (*chiragh*) of the home is a traditional term for a son.

"Then why don't you leave that blind fool? You should at least protect your own reputation. You couldn't have forgotten that couplet we learned in school, 'Seeing milk in the liquor vendor's hands, everyone thinks it is wine.'"[7]

"Oh my God," said another to Devsingh. "Just come and hear what people are saying in my neighborhood. Kalyan is disgraced on all sides. Everyone says that the shadow of Muslim poets has fallen on this Hindi poet. The idiot ignores his own culture and pure religion and runs about after 'idols.'[8] The wretch's father was a competent guy who earned and saved money otherwise the world would tear him to pieces. These days, money hides the greatest sins."

"So do talent and education," a third man piped up. "I know dozens of educated people who commit the same sin as Kalyanchandra, hiding behind their knowledge and scholarship the way he's hiding behind his money."

"Modern education draws people to such sins," said the first one. "Our ancient education system didn't make us so impure. These days, after fueling the fire for twelve years in an English school in Delhi, educated young men set out to try all the shops of sin. As soon as they learn four words of English they get up on a *white horse*, go to the *white market*, and shamelessly start sweeping the chocolate path with the broom of desire, under the veil of beauty, love, and discovery. God has not yet given me a son, but if that day comes and I think it necessary to send my son to school or college, I will shoot him before I do that. Ha, ha, ha, ha—no, don't laugh; it's not a joke. I'm absolutely convinced that our present-day educational institutions are not fit for us to rely on. We cannot send our sons—the lamps of our lineage, the fame of our families—to them without feeling nervous. In twelve years, our schools do turn their brains into museums, but because the

7. Quote from Hindi devotional poetry.

8. Quotation marks in the original. The word is *buth*, literally idol, used in Urdu poetry to refer to the beloved. Ironically, here a Hindu calls Muslims idol worshipers (*buthparast*) because of Urdu poetry's celebration of worshiping the beloved (*buth*). But the word *buthparast* originates from the Muslim view of Hindus (who worship images) as idolaters.

education system and the teacher training programs are foreign, their hearts become hellish. Oh! The meaning of education is to make life happy, but how many of the educated in our country today can purify their environment with true happiness? Very few. Almost none. I say that if I have to send my son to today's educational institutions, I will shoot and kill him."

"Enough, enough!" another interrupted. "Let us finish questioning this Devsinghji about that Kalyan.[9] You and your endless lectures against present-day educational institutions! Yes, brother, tell us one thing. Why does he love that village boy, that son of his tenant, so much? We've heard that he spends all his time adorning that boy. He doesn't even send him to school. He says he's educating him himself. He serves that boy hand and foot, even bathes him and does his hair. Why does he do all this, brother? Has Kalyan's wife died? Have all the market prostitutes gone to hell?"

"Kalyan says," replied Devsingh, "that his wife cannot respond to his love. She's not worthy of being given the priceless jewel of the heart. But that boy is exactly the god Kalyan has been looking for. He says he loves him with a pure heart. There is not even a whiff of lust in his love. Those who defame him for this love are heartless, narrow-minded in their definition of love, and completely incompetent to judge. He says he can give up his honor, his wealth, and everything else but cannot give up the love of that lad."

"He's a liar," said one man. "His love is not pure; it is lust. He and his boy are being defamed on all sides, and he puts up with it. He lets his beloved be defamed! Yuck, this is not love but blindness. As I said, he has picked this up from Urdu poets. He must be kissing and embracing that boy in the same style. Forget it — I get too worked up when I discuss these things. Since I heard this about him, I've been very careful not to come face to face with him. I'm afraid that if I meet him I may go mad with loathing. I might start beating up the wretch and asking why he does not love me. I too am a man. Why doesn't he look for his heavenly poetry in me? Rascal! He'll do . . . . and say that his love

9. The honorific *ji* is sarcastically appended to Devsingh's name.

is pure.[10] Forget it, let's go. Pardon us, Sir, we troubled you for nothing. Let the wretch die. One of these days, the pot of his sins is bound to explode. God will pay him back."

3.

There is no doubt about it, and Thakur Devsingh acknowledges to this day that Babu Kalyanchandra started off by loving that poor but beautiful boy as his own and with a pure heart. He admitted to the Thakur at the start that such love becomes infernal when it grows impure and perverted by desire. So at the outset he would gaze upon him from a distance and consider himself the equivalent of Majnun and Farhad.[11]

But later he felt that his heart was not satisfied with gazing from afar. His heart kept craving for something more and something yet more from that tender bundle of love. Gradually his being longed to blend with and be lost in the being of that boy. His heart quickly found a pretext. He began to imagine—why would it be wrong to love him, my beloved, more closely? I am not an idiot who would fall from my ideal and do anything bad. I have full confidence in myself. Yes, yes, there is no harm; I will love him more closely. Oh! What joy there is in this love, what heaven in this transaction!

Finally, he was sold down the river by his own heart and began to keep that boy close to him as often as he could. His heart, which had blossomed just by looking at him, now was gladdened by touching him, embracing him as if by accident, and brushing against different parts of his body!

One day, Kalyanchandra was sitting alone in his room, his heart throbbing with thoughts of his beloved, writing poems as he quivered

10. Ellipses in the original.

11. Two famous mythological lovers (Majnun was Laila's lover and Farhad Shirin's) from Persian poetry, who were also celebrated in Urdu poetry as types of selfless devotion.

with joy. Oh! How the poems flowed in waves from his brain! What deep feelings were seen in his lines!

As he was writing, his friend, who had gone out, came into the room. As soon as he saw him, the flow of his imagination was obstructed. His body quivered and his eyes filled with tears. He blushed and then became still. The pen fell from his hand. He called out, "Listen! Come here a minute!"

The innocent boy came and stood before him.

"Here — come sit by me. Oh! Why do you keep going off on your own? Don't you know how much I love you? Mad fellow! Why do you leave me and go away? Look at the poem I have written, thinking of you. You are still standing? Come here. No, wait! Close that door from inside. Yes, now it's all right — come."

Standing up, Kalyanchandra picked up the boy and embraced him! Began to kiss him!! Began to tremble.

That day, Kalyanchandra's heart suddenly attacked him violently. His heart made him do what until then he had never even imagined. In a moment, the pure Ganga of his love flowed out like a dirty gutter.

Love and licentiousness took hands and began to do a hellish dance of destruction in that solitary room!![12]

The poet — the ambassador of heaven — began to play the part of a demon!

4.

Gradually, the rustic boy's face began to lose its beauty. Its boyish innocence and tenderness began to be replaced by a prostitute's shamelessness and harshness. Kalyan Babu's face too began to look demonic. The other boys of the neighborhood seemed afraid when they looked at his big, dim eyes. As if those eyes spoke to them in some uncivilized language. Slowly, most of his friends became distanced from

12. The word used for dance is *tandav*, Lord Shiva's dance of destruction. Ugra refers to this divine dance as hellish and demonic.

him. If they ever ran into him, they would look away. He was now disgraced throughout the city as a person of bad character. Everyone began whispering about him. But there was not a single person in the community willing to confront him or openly denounce him. Society does not enjoy trying to uplift people as much as it does carrying tales about them.

✳ ✳ ✳ ✳   ✳ ✳ ✳ ✳   ✳ ✳ ✳ ✳   ✳ ✳ ✳ ✳

It was eight at night. The boy was out and had not yet returned, though Kalyanchandra was very restless without him. He was anxiously pacing at the door, humming a tune.

Just then, a poor old man from the neighborhood came up and gave him the news: "Brother, a terrible thing has happened. What kind of boy is that you have kept? The whole city is buzzing with it."

"What nonsense are you talking? Be quiet!" Kalyan rebuked the old man.

"Why get angry with me?" he responded. "I just came to warn you for your own good that the police will soon be coming to take care of you."

"Why? Why? Why will the police come?" Kalyan asked, somewhat alarmed.

"Because that kept fellow of yours" the old man replied, "was caught in the park, doing . . . . . . with another boy, and people beat him up badly.[13] But the testimony he gave at the police station cut your nose and your family honor off at the root. He said that you taught him that sinful act. You regularly act in that infernal way with him. He said many other things too and gave lots of evidence against you!"

5.

The day after this incident, the police knocked on Kalyanchandra's door and called out to him. But the people in his house had been per-

13. Ellipses in original.

plexed all night, because he had been missing since nine o'clock the previous night.

They began to search the whole house, and in a little while suspected that he was in a room that had been found closed. The police broke the door down and found the poet Kalyanchandra sleeping soundly in the lap of an infernal death. His face was black, and he was foaming at the mouth. He had perhaps taken poison and ended his hellish life.

The police found a letter in his pocket.

"The man responsible for the destruction of the character of the boy. . . . . . is the one in whose pocket the police find this letter. I sowed the seeds of hell in his heaven. I ignorantly blackened the page of his life. In penance for my actions I am taking poison. I am a coward and do not have the courage to face the police, the courts, and society. I pray to the ministers of justice that after reading this letter of confession they have mercy on the boy, and try to lead him towards the light. I'm going to hell to repent for my deeds. And I'm leaving a *will* for fifty thousand rupees out of my estate to be used for the boy's future. I hope that my last wish will be fulfilled.

Infernal
Kalyanchandra"

IN PRISON

1.

It was not the first of the month, nor was it the fifteenth. So I was surprised to hear the madwoman ring.[1]

"What's happening, Sukhu?" I asked a gangster prisoner who was printing blocks near me. "Why is the madwoman ringing at this time today? Has someone escaped?"

"Who knows, Baba?" Poor Sukhu expressed the simple devotion of his heart by addressing every rag-tag political prisoner, from the era of noncooperation to the time I went to prison, as "Baba." "The door is closed, or I would go ask the warder. It is still ringing. Really looks as if something has gone wrong."

I asked, "You've been doing the rounds of the jails in this district for ten years—you must know all about when the madwoman rings."

Sukhu replied, "Sure, Baba, I do, and when I first came to this hell, the first year I was here, this madwoman bothered me a lot one day. I am a blacksmith, so I did not have to stay at the grinding stone for long. As soon as the jailor became aware that I could make chairs and tables, he sent me straight to the blacksmith and carpentry section. To

This story, "*Jail Mein*," also first appeared in the book in 1927.

1. [Explanatory footnote in the original] Prisoners, especially in the United Provinces, call the alarm signal "madwoman."

test my skills, they cut a part of that *shisham* tree you see there, and I was ordered to make two chairs and a fine table. Later, I found out that Saheb liked the things I made so much that he had them sent to his bungalow."[2]

I interrupted, "What do you mean Saheb had them sent, Sukhu? Did he take them for free or did he buy them?"

"Oh, Baba, how you talk! Saheb—the superintendent—is the king of the jail. Why would he buy things made by the prisoners? He's the master of the jail, isn't he, Baba? Prisoners weave rugs for him, churn butter for him, the tailors stitch fashionable clothes for Miss Saheb, Baba, and Baby—do you think he pays for any of these things?[3] Never. But I was talking about the madwoman. Wait a bit, though. The warder is coming to count us."

The next moment, the Indian warder of our ward, in his black turban and khaki uniform, holding the bunch of keys that keeps unfortunate men locked in iron cages, was seen approaching.

"Guard," he called out to the prisoner who was his assistant. "Make them sit in pairs. Count them."

Sukhu was a hard-working craftsman and a long-time prisoner. The officers were generally pleased with him. So he could address the warders with some familiarity. He asked, "Warder Saheb, why did the madwoman ring today?"

"Sit in a pair, you nephew of a *barrister*. The madwoman rang because your father's nose got cut off!"

"You are my father, warder Saheb!" Sukhu smiled and wagged his tail before that Nawab, who earned twenty rupees a month, more ingratiatingly than flatterers of real Nawabs do.

2. "Saheb" is a British officer.

3. This interlude indicates the corruption of the British jailers and their families, who exploited the prisoners.

"Two, four, six, eight, ten, twelve, fourteen, twenty-five, eighteen, twenty-two, and I am the twenty-third!"

As soon as the poor, foolish prisoner, who had been made an overseer, and who was not very good at counting, held out the report, the warder rebuked him, "You nephew of a pig's daughter's mother's sister's granddaughter's child! The bastard does not even know how to count. If any officer heard of this, I would have to answer for it. If you count wrong again, I'll have your badge taken away. You son of a louse's brother's wife's brother's grandson! Go on and count again."

The poor prisoner overseer trembled, and began counting again: "Two, four, six, eight, ten, twelve, fourteen, sixteen, eighteen, twenty, twenty-two, and I am the twenty-third. Twenty-three prisoners, the bars, the lock, it's all right, Sir!"

Immediately, fearful shouts of "It's all right, Sir!" arose from all corners of that huge hell like the howls of jackals in the silent night. This process continued for about forty-five minutes. While it was going on, the senior warden and the junior jailer came and checked each one of us out, as if we were rupee coins. Finally, the jail superintendent, accompanied by armed warders and other staff officers, made his rounds. He heard the reports of "The prisoners are all here, Sir," and then marched off with his retinue.

Sukhu began to whisper in my ear as soon as the superintendent left. "Yes, Baba, I was telling you the story of the madwoman. Don't laugh, although I myself feel like laughing when I recall my own foolishness. I was working on a chair in the carpentry section when I heard shouts from outside of 'Madwoman! Madwoman!' The prisoners around me also stood up and began to yell, 'Madwoman! Madwoman!' I immediately picked up a piece of wood and leapt towards the gate, ready to capture the madwoman and beat her up if necessary. But later, the warder cursed me out and told me that madwoman is the prisoners' name for the frightening sound of that signal which the warder at the gate sets off to alert people."

Sukhu kept talking but I was not interested in his story. I had already guessed what silly things a simpleton like Sukhu was likely to have done when he first heard the word "madwoman." I was more interested in finding out why the madwoman had rung today.

"Warder Saheb!" This time I asked the question. "Why did the madwoman ring today?"

"Once again, prisoners fought over a boy," replied the warder. "A Pathan threw down another Muslim man and bit off his nose with his teeth."[4]

"For a boy!" I was surprised. "Are minors also kept in these prisons? Are there boys here too? Do noses get cut off and people get beaten over them here too?"

The warder replied, "Minors are not kept in this circuit, but who bothers about age in prison? Prisoners are long-time sinners. Their boys can be anything up to sixty years old. A month ago, a long-time thief came here sentenced to two years' hard time. His name is "Sundar," his caste is Bhar, and he is twenty-five years old.[5] I first saw him in Ballia—no, Sundarpur jail. There too, he used to avoid work and used to do "that act" with prisoners, thus reducing his own hard labor. Some would do the grinding for him, because he was their boy. Others would divide his burdens among themselves because he was their boy."

I asked, "Didn't you and the jail superintendent know about this?"

"Everyone knew, but even the big Saheb could get in trouble for matters concerning boys. People could lose their positions. Generally, warders were too afraid to make a fuss and kept such matters quiet."

"So what happened today?"

"As soon as Sundar came into the circuit again, a Pathan tried to make him his boy. He would secretly give him cigarettes, chewing to-

4. The word translated as "boy" throughout this story is *launda*, which literally means boy but is used, in different contexts, to refer to older males too. *Laundebaazi* (interest in boys) is one of the terms still used to refer to male homosexuality.

5. The word Sundar is in quotes in the original. Sundar means beautiful and is a male name. It is not clear if this is the prisoner's real name or a nickname.

bacco, and snacks. But another Muslim was also anxious to grab him. He too began to dance attendance on that wretched Bhar with snacks and cigarettes. This morning the Pathan told his companions, 'I'll drink that Rahim's blood. He does the bad act with my boy. He wants to take away what belongs to me.'[6] Just two hours later he bit his nose off! Now all of them are being presented before Saheb at the gate."

"What will happen now?" I asked.

"Saheb can get him caned or send him to court and have his sentence increased. He can reduce his days of remission. Maybe he'll just be caned. Let's see."

3.

That evening, after we had all eaten that wonderful food which even a dog would sniff and leave uneaten, had finished our parade, and had been counted and locked in our barracks, Sukhu told us that Saheb had ordered the Pathan to be given twenty lashes. The canes had been soaked. Tomorrow, in the Saheb's presence, a Bhangi would make the Pathan's skin, flesh, and blood fly. He also told us that the boy had been fettered in solitary confinement and would be sent to another jail in a couple of days.

I asked, "Sukhu, why do 'such acts' happen in jail? This is very bad. It means that sinners come here and become terrible sinners. Why can't this be stopped?"

"Oh, Baba," Sukhu replied. "What do you know? You have come with a four-day royal sentence; you will reign here, argue with the officers in English, and leave. Ask those who have long sentences why they do this? They are helpless; after suppressing Eros in the heart for eight, ten, twelve years, these crude prisoners, ignorant of the subtleties of purity and impurity, go mad, forget themselves and do such things.[7] This vice is very common in jails, Baba, whether it is here, in

6. "Bad act": *bura kaam.*
7. "Eros in the heart": *man ke kamdev.*

Punjab, in Bengal, or in the Andamans. This has never been stopped and never can be stopped."

"It can be stopped," I said, "but not till the government genuinely tries to reform the unfortunate prisoners. If they give the prisoners religious and humanistic education, and tell them about the dangers of sin and its harmful consequences, and try to reform them, they can succeed. But why would the government bother to do this? The government thinks it has done its duty by giving sinners harsh punishments. Fine words about reforming prisoners occur only in prison reports."

"Who's talking?" the warder asked harshly from outside, hearing our voices. Silence fell in the barracks.

As I fell asleep, I was reflecting on the fact that the pursuit of chocolate goes on right under the government's nose. The crime for which the law sends people away for years is openly committed in prisons! Delightful!

FROM *Letters of Some Beautiful Ones*

Calcutta, 19 November, 1925

Dearest,[1]

It has been two years since I last wrote you a letter. Thinking of my "dearest" after two years, numberless radiant memories awaken in my heart's dark temple. Our "beautiful past" — oh, oh!

I am writing to you, so today you will definitely appear in my

The title of this epistolary novel, *Chand Haseenon ke Khutoot* (1927), is a quote from a famous couplet often attributed to Ghalib: "*Chand tasveere-butaan, chand haseenon ke khutoot / Baad marney key merey ghar se yeh saaman nikley*" (A few pictures of idols, a few letters of beautiful ones / After my death, this is all that was found in my house), although no source has been discovered (thanks to Harish Trivedi for reminding me of this). The novel begins with a letter from a Muslim woman named Nargis, who is studying in Calcutta, to her brother's wife, Asghari, telling her that she has fallen in love with a Hindu man, Murari Krishna. The second letter, with which these translated excerpts begin, is from Murari Krishna to his friend Govind Hari Sharma, with whom he grew up in Allahabad. This translation is from the 1987 edition, published by Vani Prakashan, New Delhi.

1. Murari addresses Govind as *Priyatam* (dearest), and Govind addresses Murari as *Pyare* (beloved). These names are often used as romantic epithets between men and women.

dreams. Do come and meet me. In the same way as we used to meet in Prayag. Let it be the same kind of beautiful evening; let me come back home from studying and hurriedly wash my face and hands in my eagerness to meet "someone." Come as you used to, overflowing with love, and let us forget everything else and blossom with joy at seeing each other. Say as you used to, "Muli, hurry up."[2] I will pout and pretend to be annoyed: "Go and tell whoever is a radish to hurry up."

You: "Muli!"

I (in a rush): "You radish, you carrot, you eggplant, you pumpkin!"

You: "All right, Honorable Mister Murari Krishan Saheb, *Phonograph of India*, I appear in your presence. Satisfied now? Please hurry up. If you spend the evening here, when will we get to play?"

And I, as usual, saying, "Don't make a row, sir," throw a pillow at you. You take off your coat, cap, shirt, and throw them at me. I say, "*Hands up*"; you say, "*Hands up!*" As always, I suddenly slap your fair, full, beautiful cheek in a way that attracts the heart. You fall on me, subdue me, throw me to the ground, sit on my chest, and say, "Wicked one!" I laugh and reply, "Beloved of a wicked one!" You say, "Come on," and I say, "Let me go."

Show me all this once more in a dream, dearest! How good those days were!!

[*We learn that Murari Krishan is now a college student, while Govind Hari is involved in Congress[3] nationalist politics and has been in prison. Murari needs his advice.*]

It's a brief story. I had played a football match with the whites and was returning home when on the way I met a very beautiful girl.[4]

2. *Muli*, literally "radish," is a playful diminutive for Murari.

3. The Indian National Congress was the party that led India to independence, was in power for several decades thereafter, is still one of two leading political parties at the national level, and is in power at the time of writing.

4. *Balika*—can mean girl child or young girl. *Balak*, the male form of this word, is used to refer to the boys who are love objects in *Chocolate*. Ugra laments the exploitation of their youth, but here he does not consider the girl's youth as making her an inappropriate love object.

She was brilliant like a heap of gold and sparkled like a string of diamonds. Eyes like yours, a beautiful face like yours, a sweet smile like yours, a nose like yours, and lips like yours (if you saw her, you would cry, "Sister, sister"). I swear by your heart! I swear by your smile!!

[*A secret courtship ensues, which culminates in a kiss that Murari describes.*]

Gently pushing her beautiful nose (what can I say about whose nose it was like?), and her full red lips with my lips, I said, "I do not give answers, I ask questions."

[*When Murari discovers that Nargis is a Muslim, he gets worried, as his father is a highly orthodox Hindu Brahman, a civil servant in the British government*]

Dearest, we had vowed that we would consult each other before getting married. I need you desperately now. Come here for a few days if you can. . . .

If you come to Calcutta, be prepared to lose your dharma. Because I have kissed a Muslim woman and you will have to kiss me.

Your
agitated
Murari Krishan

[*In his reply, Govind Hari recalls how Murari's father objected to their friendship because Govind is from a poor family. Afraid that Govind would draw Murari into Gandhi's civil disobedience movement, Murari's father, a British loyalist, sent Murari off to Calcutta. Govind went to prison a couple of times, hence their separation for two years.*]

Beloved Murari,
[. . .]
You disliked your father's ideas as much as I did. Because "I" was you; "you" were me. Because I was "dearest" [*priyatam*] and you were "beloved" [*pyare*]. Because I was the dawn and you the young sun. Because I was the gentle moist breeze and you the perfumed spring

breeze. Because I was the lips and you a kiss.[5] Because we flowed in one wave, spoke with one voice, sang to one tune, danced to one beat. You were "I," and "I" was "you." The maker of your flesh and blood, the owner of your flesh and blood, wanted to forcibly hold your heart in his fist. He could not bear the thought of a poor unfortunate like me enjoying immortality by holding to my breast the plaything that he had made.

[Govind recalls Murari's own regret at being unable to be with Govind in prison and share his trials. He quotes from a letter Murari had written to him while he was in prison.]

"I am base, mean, a coward. I cannot share your tribulations, even though you are the life of my life. . . . I constantly pray to God to give me the strength to respectfully but fearlessly oppose my honored father when the need arises. I swear by your love, I will consider myself blessed when I attain that strength. And then I will not leave your shadow, in life, in death, in travel, in battle, in prosperity, in difficulty, in prison, and at the gallows.[6] Even today, you are the creator of my heart's purity, you are the Himachal mountain from which the Ganga of my heart flows."

[Govind recounts his recent meeting with Murari's parents. They encouraged him to marry, but when he told them he would marry a woman of his own choice, who might be a widow, or belong to another caste or religion, Murari's father got very angry and said he would disown his son if he did such a thing.]

I have definitely decided to come to Calcutta. But you have invited me to lose my dharma and take a kiss. I have to come prepared to accept this invitation. I am fresh from my in-laws' house, the residence of my wife, the bureaucracy.[7] My beard has grown out like Rasputin's. My hair is matted. You are emotional, a worshiper of beauty, a narcis-

5. This series of coupled metaphors adheres to a premodern convention of love poetry, which continues to inform modern Hindi film songs, in which two lovers are figured as complementary and paired natural forces.

6. This line clearly echoes marriage vows.

7. Joking reference to prison.

sus creeper—how can you accept my long beard? So I am making myself somewhat "smooth" as soon as possible and am coming into your arms.[8]

[The last letter is from Govind Hari to the editor of the Kanpur-based newspaper Pratap, *who had commissioned him to write a story on the Calcutta riots, since he was going there to meet Murari. Here, he describes how he found Murari, who was killed by Muslim rioters, led by Yaqub, his rival for Nargis's love.]*

My friend asked, "Panditji, do you recognize that girl? She looks exactly like you."

Exactly like me! I remembered the words in my beloved Murari's letter: "Eyes like yours, a beautiful face like yours, a sweet smile like yours, a nose like yours, and lips like yours."

[Govind leaps out of the moving car, injuring his knees, and jumps into the police ambulance to see the corpse.]

That face was covered with a cloth, which I removed. That face was covered with wounds made by fearful weapons. That face was covered with numberless streams of blood. Even though lifeless, that face spoke of honor and courage, happiness and love. I immediately recognized that beautiful and beloved face, even though it was so distorted. Oh! Immediately.

It was the same face that I had gazed upon—gazed upon—gazed upon, with ever-eager eyes at the dawn of my life. It was the same face on seeing which the driest bud in my heart used to grow green and blossom. It was the same face, just a glimpse of which used to set the heavenly voice of my inner being in motion. It was the same face whose beauty I had once considered the beauty of Tulsidas's face that "put to shame a thousand lotuses."[9] It was the same face that was my heaven, my liberation, my gladness, my ideal, my well-being, my life. It was the same face—it was the same face!

I was paralyzed by the terrible condition of that heart of my heart,

8. The word for "smooth" is *chikna.* Saleem Kidwai points out that this word is commonly used even today to describe the beauty of a male youth.

9. Tulsidas's description of Shri Ram's beautiful face.

that life of my life. I lost my senses. I did not know what I should or should not do. A terrible tempest of different emotions arose all at once in my heart. I felt anger—at the murderers of my dearest—like an angry ocean, a raging fire, a volcano spitting out flames. I felt compassion—at that condition of my beloved—like the heart of a widow, like the lament of a mother, like Dasharatha deprived of Rama. I don't know how long I remained, almost unconscious in the ambulance, kneeling by my dearest one's corpse. I neither wept nor laughed, neither trembled nor moved.

[Nargis, who is very disturbed and agitated, raves against Islam and declares that she is a Hindu. She refuses to return home with her father and insists on staying with Govind as his sister, saying she wants to travel, preaching against Muslim culture.]

PANDEY BECHAN SHARMA "UGRA" (Extreme), 1900–1967, was a nationalist writer, jailed twice by the British. He edited and wrote for many newspapers, authored several novels and short story collections, and was dubbed a founder of the genre of *ghaslet* (inflammatory literature). He lived in Benaras, Calcutta, Bombay (where he wrote film scripts), and Delhi. He never married.

RUTH VANITA, professor at the University of Montana, former reader at Delhi University, India, was founding co-editor of *Manushi* from 1978 to 1990. She is the author of *Love's Rite: Same-Sex Marriage in India and the West* (Palgrave 2005), *Gandhi's Tiger and Sita's Smile: Essays on Gender, Culture and Sexuality* (Yoda 2005), *Sappho and the Virgin Mary: Same-Sex Love and the English Literary Imagination* (Columbia 1996; Indian edition 2007), and *A Play of Light: Selected Poems* (Penguin 1994). She edited, *Queering India: Same-Sex Love and Eroticism in Indian Culture and Society* (Routledge 2002) and, with Saleem Kidwai, *Same-Sex Love in India: Readings from Literature and History* (St. Martin's 2000). She has translated many works of fiction and poetry from Hindi and Urdu to English, and published essays on Shakespeare in several journals, most recently in *Shakespeare Survey*, 2007.

Library of Congress Cataloging-in-Publication Data
Sharma, Pande Bechan, 1901–1967
[Short stories. English. Selections]
Chocolate and other writings on male homoeroticism /
by Pandey Bechan Sharma "Ugra";
translated and with an introduction by Ruth Vanita.
p. cm.
Includes bibliographical references.
ISBN 978-0-8223-4361-5 (cloth : alk. paper)
ISBN 978-0-8223-4382-0 (pbk. : alk. paper)
1. Sharma, Pande Bechan, 1901–1967—Translations into English.
2. Male homosexuality—Fiction. 3. Male homosexuality in literature.
I. Vanita, Ruth. II. Title.
PK2098.S468A2 2009
891.4'336—dc22   2008048030